John Creasey – Master Storyteller

C000079034

Born in Surrey, England in 1908
there were nine children, John Creasey grew up to be a true master story teller and international sensation. His more than 600 crime, mystery and thriller titles have now sold 80 million copies in 25 languages. These include many popular series such as *Gideon of Scotland Yard*, *The Toff*, *Dr Palfrey* and *The Baron*.

Creasy wrote under many pseudonyms, explaining that booksellers had complained he totally dominated the 'C' section in stores. They included:

> *Gordon Ashe, M E Cooke, Norman Deane, Robert Caine Frazer, Patrick Gill, Michael Halliday, Charles Hogarth, Brian Hope, Colin Hughes, Kyle Hunt, Abel Mann, Peter Manton, J J Marric, Richard Martin, Rodney Mattheson, Anthony Morton and Jeremy York.*

Never one to sit still, Creasey had a strong social conscience, and stood for Parliament several times, along with founding the One Party Alliance which promoted the idea of government by a coalition of the best minds from across the political spectrum.

He also founded the British Crime Writers' Association, which to this day celebrates outstanding crime writing. The Mystery Writers of America bestowed upon him the *Edgar Award* for best novel and then in 1969 the ultimate *Grand Master* Award. John Creasey's stories are as compelling today as ever.

INPECTOR WEST SERIES

The Case Against
Paul Raeburn

(Triumph for Inspector West)

John Creasey

HOUSE OF
STRATUS

This edition published in 2009 by House of Stratus, an imprint of Stratus Books Ltd., Lisandra House, Fore St., Looe, Cornwall, PL13 1AD, UK.

www.houseofstratus.com

Typeset by House of Stratus.

A catalogue record for this book is available from the British Library and the Library of Congress.

ISBN 0755I-1769-7
EAN 978-07551-1769-7

CHAPTER I

A LITTLE MAN DIES

THE POWERFUL car moved swiftly and quietly along the road which led across Clapham Common. The beams of its headlights caught the grass and trees, making them a vivid green. It was nearly one o'clock in the morning, and the driver had not seen a soul since he had turned on to the Common road. He was humming under his breath.

Suddenly a man appeared.

The driver saw him dart forward, and took his foot off the accelerator. The man stopped in the middle of the road, his feet wide apart, his hands held above his head. The driver trod heavily on the brake and the car jolted to a standstill. As he did so, the man who had caused the emergency came quickly towards the car, and opened the door.

"Well, well," he said in a sneering voice, "if it isn't Mr Raeburn. The great Paul Raeburn himself! How's it going, Mr Raeburn?"

In the light from the dashboard, his face showed thin and pale. His hands, gripping the side of the door, were white. Despite the sneer, his nervousness was unmistakable.

The driver showed no signs of nerves. "Who are you, and what's this all about?" he demanded.

"What a question to ask, Mr Raeburn," jeered the little man. "You don't forget your old friends as easily as all that, surely. Just think back a few years. Perhaps it will help you if I say 'Southampton'. You ought to have a good memory." He now sounded breathless, as if he had been running. "Driving about in a Rolls, too. You've come up in the world, haven't you?"

The driver took a cigarette case from his pocket.

"You're Halliwell," he said in a flat voice.

"Well, isn't that marvellous!" exclaimed Halliwell. "You've remembered your old pal! You didn't think I was alive, did you, Paul? You thought you were safe from me, but what a mistake. Supposing you get out and we have a little chat?"

"Supposing you get in beside me."

"I'm not falling for any tricks like that, Paul," Halliwell said. "I'm older and much smarter than I was, and I want a chat with you."

Raeburn sat quite still, watching the other, seeing the indications that Halliwell had screwed himself up to a great pitch to do this. He had a pinched, hungry look and his eyes were watering.

Then, suddenly:

"How much do you want?" Raeburn asked.

"How much do I want?" Halliwell stretched out his hand and clutched Raeburn's wrist. "That's easy to answer. I want half of everything. I'm after a fifty-fifty partnership. I'm going into partnership with a millionaire! You are a millionaire, Paul, aren't you? One of the great 'I ams'. But if I were to tell all I know, where would you be?"

"You wouldn't do that, would you?" asked Raeburn softly.

Halliwell began to laugh, but the laugh turned into a fit of coughing. Raeburn waited, quite impassively, but his fingers were tight on the cigarette case. Once he raised it, like a club.

Some distance ahead, the wavering light of a cycle appeared; Halliwell was still coughing when the cyclist passed, but soon managed to speak again.

"I'm going to have my share back, they're my only terms – full partnership, or I talk. I've served my sentence, three bloody years in jail. Years you owe me, Paul. If I talk, nothing else can happen to me, I've paid in full, but you – well, just you think about it."

"I'm thinking," Raeburn said. "Get in, and we'll go to my flat and have a drink."

"We'll talk where I want to," insisted Halliwell. "I've worked it all out, to the last comma. I've watched you night after night, driving across the Common. Do you know I didn't recognise you at first? I saw the Rolls, and used to think if my partner had acted rightly by me I'd be in a car like that. Then I recognised you, and saw how right I was."

"If you won't come and talk it over, I can't help you," Raeburn said flatly.

"You'll come and talk with me," said Halliwell "I'll give you my address, and I'll have some friends as witnesses. Don't think you'll get away with anything but a partnership, Paul."

Raeburn said: "We'll see about that." He flipped open the cigarette case and pushed it under Halliwell's nose, and Halliwell backed away in alarm. Raeburn glanced into the driving mirror, and saw no light reflected on it. He leaned out, and punched Halliwell savagely in the stomach, bringing his head forward; then he struck Halliwell behind the ear with a corner of the case. Halliwell grunted, and slumped against the car. Raeburn pushed him away, and he fell, dazed if not unconscious.

Raeburn turned off the headlights, stabbed the self-starter, slapped the gear into reverse, and drove the Rolls back a few yards, until the sidelights picked out Halliwell's face, and even showed the mark of bleeding just behind his ear.

Raeburn moistened his lips as he looked at the offside wheel, then at Halliwell's head. He clenched his teeth, put the car into forward gear and trod on the accelerator. The Rolls Royce surged forward, and jolted.

Raeburn changed gear and drove on, his lips still set very tightly, and he stared into the driving mirror. He saw no light; nor did he see a little man with a wriggly nose, who appeared from some bushes near the spot where murder had been done; he did not look at Halliwell, just stared after the disappearing car.

The man began to walk in the other direction, smiling faintly. The Common seemed completely deserted, until a cyclist appeared, fifty yards in front of him. The little man moved back into the shadows, and drew in his breath sharply when he saw a policeman's uniform.

Several nights a week, Paul Raeburn drove from a club near the Common to his Park Lane flat. When feeling in the mood, he would drive for twenty miles out of London and return along the deserted roads, revelling in the speed of his car and the power under his control. It was a kind of relaxation. Tonight, he drove to Battersea, crossed the Thames and swung the car left, towards Fulham and Putney. Once at the top of Putney Hill, he turned towards Roehampton. Little traffic was about. Now and again he saw a policeman and his lips tightened, but his hands were steady.

Near Roehampton he pulled into the side of the road, leaned over to the back of the car, and took a flask from a pocket behind his seat. He unscrewed the cap, and put the mouth of the flask to his lips. He took three or four gulps, then took the flask away, and screwed on the cap.

He took out his cigarette case, lit a cigarette and examined each corner of the case; there was a faint red stain on one.

He got out of the car, wiped the case on the grass, slipped it back into his pocket, tossed the cigarette away, and took the wheel again. He sat still, thinking intently, then moved suddenly, rubbed his pigskin gloves over the door where Halliwell had touched it.

He was reversing when he saw the headlights of a car coming from Roehampton, and was in the middle of the road when he noticed the blue-and-white sign: POLICE.

He waved the driver on. The police car passed, only to swing across his hood. He put on the brakes, staring at the two uniformed policemen who jumped out and hurried back.

He opened his window.

"Good evening, sir," said one of the men. "Are you Mr Paul Raeburn?"

"Eh?" On the instant Raeburn's voice became thick and hoarse, and he looked bleary-eyed as he peered at the man. "Whassat?"

"I said, are you Mr Paul Raeburn?"

"'S'my name. No business of yours." Raeburn hiccupped.

4

"Every right to drive if – hic – I want to."

"Of course you have, sir," said the policeman, soothingly. "You're not feeling well, are you?"

"Feel wunnerful," muttered Raeburn. "Wunnerful party – hic. Want to go home."

"I think; if you don't mind, I'll drive you," said the policeman, with careful politeness. "You don't want another accident, do you?"

"'Nother what?" asked Raeburn, thickly. "Never had an accident in my life! Clean record – hic." He glared at the man, who began to push him to the other side of the car. "Oh, well, drive the dam' thing if you want to."

When the car pulled up outside Clapham Police Station, half an hour later, Raeburn was breathing heavily, and seemed to be asleep or in a stupor.

Chief Inspector Roger West, in shirtsleeves and without a collar and tie, was having breakfast in the kitchen of his Chelsea home. The kitchen was warm because the domestic boiler was roaring away while Roger read the *Morning Cry* and devoured sausages, bubble-and-squeak and scrambled egg. In the scullery, a daily woman was washing up; upstairs, Janet West was in the bedroom shared by their two sons, who had left for school half an hour ago.

West's fair hair was untidy, and his careless, casual air gave an almost swashbuckling look to a face which earned him his nickname: 'Handsome'. The telephone bell rang in the hall, and West finished a paragraph about a film star and her husbands, went out, and called: "I'll answer it," and went into the front room, where the telephone was on a table near his large armchair. It rang again as he sat on the arm.

"West speaking."

"It's the Yard, sir. Mr Turnbull would like a word with you."

"Put him through," said Roger.

He reached forward for a cigarette from a packet left on the table the previous night. He could reach the cigarettes but not the matches near them, and his lighter was in his coat pocket in the kitchen. He put the receiver down and grabbed the matches, and was striking one when he heard Turnbull's powerful voice.

"Handsome?"

"Can't it wait until tomorrow? I promised myself a day off."

"This won't keep for five minutes." Turnbull seldom allowed himself to be excited, but he did now. "We've got something you've been waiting for since the year Methuselah was born. Paul Raeburn's under arrest."

Roger said: "Say that again."

Turnbull spoke with great deliberation: "Paul Raeburn's-under-arrest."

Roger drew on the cigarette, and rested it carefully on an ash tray. He could hear Turnbull speaking impatiently to someone in the office; Turnbull was impatient by nature. Roger stared at the fireplace, his lips set and his eyes half closed.

Turnbull's voice became loud again. "Are you still there? Did you get it?"

"Yes, I got it," said Roger. "It isn't April 1st."

"It isn't a joke, either. Raeburn ran over a man on Clapham Common last night. A divisional copper found the body. He'd seen Raeburn's Rolls pass him near the Common, and had stopped because of trouble with his lamp. He says he thinks the Rolls stopped after the collision, and then went on. The copper knew the Rolls belonged to Raeburn, who was picked up an hour or so afterward blind drunk." Turnbull was still elated. "They kept him at Clapham overnight. We've got the swine on a hit-and-run-charge. Better than nothing anyhow."

"Undoubtedly," said Roger, but none of Turnbull's excitement sounded in his voice. "Who did he knock down?"

"We haven't identified the poor devil yet," said Turnbull. "We'll get Raeburn for manslaughter, though, it's in the bag. No doubt that it was his car, there's blood on the offside wheel and a splash or two underneath the wing. He was on the Common about the time of the accident, too. How about it?"

"Where's the body?"

"At the Clapham morgue," Turnbull answered. "You sound as if it couldn't matter less."

"Just remembering all I know about Raeburn," Roger said, carefully. "Sure it was manslaughter?"

"What do you mean?"

"It's not like Raeburn to be tight at the wheel, and he's a better than average driver," Roger replied. "Ask Gubby if he can go and see the body at once, will you? I'll be there in half an hour's time. And – are you listening?"

"Yes, but—"

"Never mind the 'buts'." Roger was suddenly sharper. "Get that dead man identified, and go all out to find evidence that he and Raeburn were acquainted. Have you tried Records yet?"

"No." Turnbull sounded subdued.

"Try 'em, and ring me at Clapham," said Roger, briskly. "Get hold of the doctor who examined Raeburn and certified him as drunk last night, too, and trace Raeburn's movements for the earlier part of the evening."

"See what you're driving at," conceded Turnbull. "Never satisfied, are you? But I can answer the last question off the cuff. He'd been to a little club near Clapham Common, The Daytime. Had plenty to drink, too."

"Raeburn has quite a reputation for holding his liquor," Roger said. "I want you, personally, to go through everything we get on the dead man as if this were a murder case. Has Raeburn sent for legal aid?"

"Yes. Abel Melville."

"Don't give Melville an inch of rope," warned Roger, urgently. "If there's any trouble, get Abbott cracking. Abbott's about the only man who can really freeze Melville." He paused, and then went on almost like a machine. "By twelve o'clock, I want to see the copper who found the body, and to know the name of everyone who was on the Common about one o'clock last night. Ask the Division chaps to give it priority. Then check at The Daytime, to find out if Raeburn had really been drinking heavily. Try to find at least two people who'll say he was sober when he left. Okay?"

"Slave driver," Turnbull growled. "I'll fix it."

"I'll be seeing you," said Roger.

He rang off, and put the cigarette between his lips; it had burned half way down, and he had to draw several times to get it going again. In his mind's eye was a picture of Paul Raeburn, smiling, handsome and self-assured.

Roger stood up, and the door opened and Janet came in.

"Got to go?"

"'Fraid so," Roger said. "I never did believe I'd get a whole day off, anyhow." He moved, slid an arm round her waist, and squeezed. "Big stuff, poppet."

"It would come today. How big, darling?"

"Paul Raeburn."

"If you had two wives, you wouldn't stay home if it's Raeburn," Janet said, resignedly.

Roger stood her away from him, and studied her for a moment; his gaze moved from her dark hair, with some grey to add a touch of distinction, to her clear grey-green eyes, and to her face. Not every man would call her beautiful, but he did. Then his eyes glinted, he glanced at the V of her green jumper, poked a finger down, as swift as lightning, and said: "If I had two wives, I'd never be home at all."

He hurried upstairs for his coat and collar and tie.

CHAPTER II

A CHANCE IN A THOUSAND

ROGER LOOKED up from the badly mutilated corpse into the eyes of Gubby Dering, a Home Office pathologist who was fast making a name for himself. Gubby was cheerful, a rotund man, with thick iron-grey hair, and horn-rimmed glasses which partly hid his grey eyes.

"Well?" asked Roger.

"No murder to prove."

"Not a hope?"

"The safe thing is to assume that it's what it seems, accidental death," Gubby told him. "The offside, wheel of the car went over the top of the head, and the legs were crushed by the other wheel. There's a small wound just behind the right ear which I can't make out, it might have been made by something projecting from the car."

"What kind of a wound?" asked Roger.

"Have a look," said Gubby, and pointed.

Roger had to bend down to see. "It might have been done just before or just after death, but you can't hope to say which." He sounded disappointed.

"I'll consult Haddon, but don't think you'll have any luck," Gubby said. "Apart from that, you'll have to accept medical evidence that the wheel crushed the top of his head, and was the direct cause of death. I saw him less than an hour after he'd been found, and he was still warm. The stomach and intestines are quite normal. He'd had a meal of fried fish, probably about two hours before death. No sign of contamination."

"Drink?"

"Whisky."

"Much?"

"Probably a couple of doubles, but I don't see what that matters," Gubby added. "Raeburn had been drinking the whisky, hadn't he?"

"If we believe all we're told, Raeburn was drunk, ran this fellow down, and didn't trouble to report it." Roger shrugged, and added dryly: "But I don't believe all I'm told. I've checked up on Raeburn so often that I can almost tell what he does every minute of the day. I know his habits, I know what he likes for supper, and I know the kind of bed warmer he likes best." Roger gave a short laugh. "I've never had a report which suggests that he ever drank too much, and I've never known him even slightly tipsy. He isn't the sort. And if he wasn't drunk, I don't believe he'd drive on after running a man down by accident."

"Deadeye Dick, the detective with a difference. Neat theory, Handsome, but I wouldn't bank on it."

"I can bank on one thing," Roger declared. "The Yard's going to work overtime for a month so as to pin another on him while he's waiting for the charge of manslaughter. If the Legal Department's awake, it'll stop him from getting bail. See Haddon soon, won't you? I'd like to know for certain if that ear injury was caused by the car, or whether there's a ghost of a chance of proving that it was from a blow received before death."

"I'll do what I can," promised Gubby. "Where are you off to?"

"The Yard," said Roger. "I've one or two people to interview."

"One or two!" jeered the pathologist. "There's probably a 'full house' notice on the waiting-room door." He offered cigarettes as he added: "You'd give your right hand to get Raeburn, wouldn't you?"

"I'd give a lot," affirmed Roger, quietly. "I think Raeburn's the ugliest piece of work I've come across in years, and what he doesn't know about making money dishonestly wouldn't cover his thumbnail. If he's not involved in a dozen rackets, I'm losing my grip. Thanks for the help," he added briskly. "Can I give you a lift?"

"No, thanks," said Gubby, "my car's outside."

As he drove across Clapham Common, Roger gave little thought to his driving, but a great deal to Raeburn. He turned into the gateway of Scotland Yard, acknowledging the salute of the two policemen on duty, and pulled up in the parking place near the steps. He did not get out at once, but sat looking towards the Embankment and watching the traffic whirling past. He was about to open the car door when Big Ben boomed the quarter.

"A quarter past eleven." He checked his watch, and found it half a minute fast. He hurried out of the car and up the steps, and as he walked along the cold stone passages, he passed several CID men.

"Now you're all right, Handsome," one called.

Roger grinned.

He entered his own office, a large, square room with big windows overlooking the Embankment. There were five yellow desks here, and his was at the back, near the window. Although it was a warm, bright day for October, a coal fire burned sluggishly in the grate.

From a desk in front of his, Chief Inspector Eddie Day looked up.

"Morning, Handsome."

"Hallo, Eddie!"

"Pretty pleased with yourself this morning, aren't you?" asked Eddie, with a sniff. "Some people have all the luck. You've been trying to pin something on Raeburn for a couple of years, now the silly mug goes and gets himself caught on a manslaughter job. They ought to call you Lucky, not Handsome."

Roger chuckled. "All right, Eddie. Have you seen Turnbull lately?"

"He's with the AC, I think," said Eddie. "That reminds me, the AC rang up twice for you. You ought to get in earlier. One of these days you'll catch a packet for not being in when he wants you."

"I dare say you're right," said Roger. He sat down and pulled the telephone towards him, and when the exchange answered, he said:

"Put me on to the Assistant Commissioner."

As he waited, he glanced at a pile of reports on the desk. Then he heard Sir Guy Chatworth's voice.

"Hallo West?"

"Good morning, sir."

"Come along right away, will you?"

"Right away, sir."

"Bit sharp, wasn't he?" asked Eddie, hopefully, as Roger replaced the receiver.

"Proper bit my head off," Roger said, solemnly.

Chatworth's room, on the second floor, was unique in the history of the Yard. The furniture was made of black glass, chromium and tubular steel, and had a cold, unfriendly look. Yet no one could be friendlier than Chatworth when he was in the mood. Just now, he was talking to Turnbull, who was sitting in one of those tubular steel chairs. Turnbull was a big, handsome man, with ruddy complexion and auburn hair; a bold, self-assured man, too.

Chatworth was also big and burly, with a fringe of grizzled curly hair at his temples and at the back of his head; the top of his head was completely bald and glistened in the light from the window. He had round, heavy features; deep grooves ran from lips to chin, and his jowl hid part of his stiff collar and tie. He was dressed that morning in a suit of shapeless brown tweed.

"Come in, and pull up a chair," he invited. "As you weren't here, I sent for Turnbull over this Halliwell business."

Roger stopped, with a hand on cold steel.

"Who, sir?"

"The dead man, Halliwell. He served three years for fraud, and had been out about three months."

Turnbull was grinning.

"I can guess what you'll think about that," Chatworth remarked, as Roger sat down. "If Raeburn is what you think, he'd have good reason for killing any man who could shop him. So I want you and Turnbull to concentrate on Raeburn, but don't let it get round that you think it might be anything but manslaughter. The Legal Department doesn't think we can get him remanded in custody, but at least you've an opportunity to dig."

"I'll dig deep," promised Roger. "Where's the Rolls now, sir?"

"At the Clapham Police Station," Turnbull answered.

"Wonder if it's been run over for prints. I ought to have checked while I was there," Roger said, aloud. "The constable who found Halliwell said that he thought the car stopped, didn't he?"

"Yes," Turnbull said.

"So Halliwell might have been in the car, and if he had, his fingerprints might be on it." Roger shook his head. "That would be too good to be true. Any special instructions, sir?"

"Yes," said Chatworth. "Prove the manslaughter case, whatever you do. Don't let Raeburn get away with this."

"Not if I can help it," Roger said, fervently.

He left the AC's office with Turnbull, spent ten minutes checking what had been done, then went down to his car again, and drove to Clapham. And still only Raeburn was on his mind, for Raeburn was not just another suspect: Raeburn was an obsession, a man with a great capacity for evil.

Arkwright, the constable who had found Halliwell, stood in front of Roger at the Clapham Police Station, holding his helmet in his hands. He was young and intelligent-looking, although obviously nervous.

"What made you think the Rolls Royce stopped?" asked Roger.

Arkwright was safe with that question. "Well, sir, first time I saw the car the headlights were on. I'd just turned on to the Common. The road's a bit twisty, and my lamp wasn't working properly, some dynamo trouble. I couldn't see much, because of the trees and bushes, but I noticed that the headlamps went out, although I could see the rear light. I said to myself the driver was in trouble, and I was going to see if I could lend a hand when my lamp went right out, so I had to get off and get it working again. If only I'd known "

Roger grinned. "No one gave me second sight, either."

Arkwright looked as if he could purr. "You know how it is when you're doing a job like that, sir," he went on. "It might have taken me a minute to fix the lamp, or it might have taken me five. I managed to get a little light, and started off again. The headlights came on just after that, so I said to myself he's all right again. I wouldn't like to *swear* that he stopped and got out, but I'm pretty sure."

"Pity, but it's a lucky thing you got what you did," said Roger. "Meet anyone else on the Common?"

"A cyclist went by just as I was turning off the main road," answered Arkwright. "I certainly didn't see anyone else until the car had disappeared and I was across the Common."

Roger let him talk for a couple of minutes, and then sent him off. Immediately, a sergeant came in to report that Dr Anstruther Breem was waiting downstairs. Breem was the doctor who had been called in to examine Raeburn at the station. He was tall, well-dressed, suave, and determined not to be over impressed by Chief Inspector West. Yes, in his opinion Raeburn had certainly been incapable of driving. He had not been able to walk along a straight line, his pronunciation of simple words had been distorted, and his breath had smelt strongly of whisky.

"He was undoubtedly drunk, Chief Inspector." Breem held a cigarette between his fingers, and his eyes were half closed.

"Could you swear that he wasn't putting on an act?" asked Roger.

"I do assure you that I know when a man is drunk."

"Yes, of course," said Roger, politely. "Thank you, Dr Breem."

Back at the Yard, he went down to the canteen with Turnbull, who had only one piece of news. Halliwell had owned a wholesale grocery business in Southampton and had set fire to warehouses which he had claimed held ten thousand pounds worth of canned and packet goods. The police had proved both arson and fraud.

"He was lucky to get away with three years," Turnbull declared.

"Yes. You'd better go to Southampton, be pleasant to the local police, and find out what you can about Halliwell's general activities," Roger said." I'll tackle The Daytime, and the people who were there last night."

The telephone bell rang, and he picked up the receiver, listened, grunted thanks, and banged it down. "Raeburn's been remanded on bail for eight days, on two sureties of five hundred pounds," he said grimly. "Get going, Warren."

The Daytime Club in Clapham had twice been raided by the police, without results, although undoubtedly gaming and drinking after licensed hours went on. Ostensibly it was owned by a syndicate, but actually Paul Raeburn owned it. Roger knew that Raeburn owned many similar clubs, but his name did not appear.

Members of The Daytime staff, who had been on duty the previous night and during the early hours of the twenty-third of October, gave Roger no help. Some said they thought Raeburn had been mixing his drinks, others were sure that he had drunk very little. Statements from members who had been present were equally contradictory.

Raeburn left London on the afternoon of the twenty-fourth and stayed at a hotel in Guildford; the local police watched his movements. Roger made several calls at the millionaire's Park Lane flat, where Warrender, Raeburn's secretary, and Ma Beesley, his housekeeper, were outwardly anxious to help, but actually evasive. Neither of them had been at The Daytime on the night of the 'accident'. They said they had never heard of Halliwell, and asserted that as far as they knew Raeburn had never done business in Southampton.

Turnbull telephoned a negative report from Southampton next morning.

Roger went over Raeburn's known record with a patience which was wearing thin, looking for the odd factor of importance that he might have missed.

Raeburn had first become prominent four years ago, as the owner of several greyhound racing tracks. The first time Roger had suspected him of criminal activity was after a series of dopings and an outcry among backers and bookmakers. No case had been proved, but the Yard had become very interested in Raeburn. He was wealthy, and had been wealthy before he had opened his greyhound tracks. He had bought small house property in country and coastal areas when it was cheap, and sold at a large profit. He had dealt first in land, then in various commodities, but no groceries. He had soon prospered enough to buy several provincial newspapers; it was freely rumoured that he was now the chief shareholder in The Cry Newspapers, Ltd., proprietor of the *Morning Cry* and the *Evening Cry*, each of which had a mammoth circulation. Recently he had bought up small circuits of provincial theatres and cinemas, owned several super-cinemas in London, and was behind two large independent television companies. Odds-on pools were his, and everything he touched made money.

One very interesting factor emerged: Among Raeburn's acquaintances were several men, rather like Halliwell, who had been caught and convicted of insurance and other frauds. The latest to be caught was a builder who had dreamed up a brilliantly clever scheme to defraud building societies. This man had done a great deal of work for Raeburn, but always on licence. The builder was not capable, in the Yard's opinion, of organising the fraud; he was simply a' front. The same was true of many of the other men, but the police always came up against a blank wall, and invariably the wall seemed to be built around Raeburn.

His legitimate interests were controlled by Raeburn Investments Limited. Warrender was Secretary of the company, and its Legal Adviser was Abel Melville, an expert in company and criminal law. Such a man could advise Raeburn just how far he could go without running into trouble.

"But he won't get Raeburn off this manslaughter charge," Turnbull declared, on the day before the second hearing. "He'll get six months or a year."

Roger made no comment.

Before going to court, he went over every piece of evidence, and then reported to Chatworth.

"Think we're all right?" the AC asked.

"Short of a miracle, we'll get him committed to the Old Bailey, sir," said Roger. "I don't think there'll be much difficulty after that. But I've drawn a blank with everything else. It's certain that two or three people were on the Common that night, but we can't get tabs on anyone. If we could prove that the car stopped—"

"Just get him on this charge," Chatworth advised. "Stop worrying about any other."

There was little choice, but Roger was uneasy when he went to court. The case had aroused a lot of interest, big crowds were gathered outside, and the public gallery was packed with friends and acquaintances of the millionaire. Roger's disquiet increased when he saw Melville smiling confidently, and Raeburn as immaculate and self-assured as ever.

Roger was with Turnbull just before the preliminaries, when the door of the room set aside for the police burst open and Eddie Day rushed in.

"'Andsome, you 'eard?" Excitement always made Eddie falter on his aspirates.

"Heard what?" demanded Roger.

"They've got a surprise witness, a girl named Franklin – some dame, too. No wonder Melville's grinning all over his face!"

That sent Roger's spirits to a record low.

CHAPTER III

SURPRISE WITNESS

MELVILLE WAS a big, round-faced man, with sleek dark hair and tufts of dark eyebrows which gave him a comical appearance. His voice was soft and seemed friendly. He sat patiently until evidence of arrest and other formalities were over; when Roger took the oath, his smile broadened and he rubbed his hands together.

Roger gave his evidence concisely to a hushed court. Raeburn's friends took in every word, obviously impressed, and once or twice even Raeburn looked anxious. But nothing disturbed Melville.

He rose to his feet as Roger finished. "I wonder if I may put one or two questions to the witness, Your Worship?"

"You may, Mr Melville."

"Thank you, sir." Melville stood in front of the witness box, still rubbing his hands together. "Knowing your excellent reputation, Chief Inspector, I take it for granted that on behalf of the police you exerted yourself in every way to endeavour to find an eyewitness of this occurrence?"

"I did," said Roger.

"Did you succeed?"

"No."

"Did you succeed in finding anyone who was on Clapham Common at the time the incident occurred?"

"Yes," said Roger.

"May I ask if you intend to produce that person as a witness?"

"Yes."

"And may I ask who he – or she – is?" went on Melville, with a glance at the magistrate.

"Is that necessary, since we are told that the person will be called to give evidence?" interrupted the magistrate.

"I think perhaps we shall progress more rapidly if the witness would answer the question," said Melville.

"Very well – you may proceed."

Roger said: "A police constable was cycling across the Common about the time of the incident."

"A police constable. I see. Wasn't it a remarkable coincidence that a constable should happen to be on the Common at the crucial time – unless, of course, he was patrolling in the course of his duty? Is that the explanation?"

"He was returning from duty," said Roger, coldly.

"Did he actually see the car?"

The magistrate leaned forward. "The witness will be able to answer for himself, Mr Melville."

"Of course, Your Worship, of course. I am considering only the precious time of the court," said Melville smoothly. "Setting aside the question of the fortuitous advent of the policeman who – er – happened to be crossing the Common at this time, but did not see what occurred, did you find any other person who was near the scene at the time?"

"No," answered Roger.

"Remarkable!" Melville actually allowed his voice to rise, and turned to the magistrate. "Your Worship, I think I should state at this juncture that there was an eyewitness of the unhappy occurrence. The police were unable to find the person, but the task presented no insuperable difficulty to the defence. I propose, with your permission, to call this witness, because I believe it can be proved that there is no case to answer."

"I will hear the evidence for the prosecution, Mr Melville."

"As you wish, Your Worship. I have no further questions to ask the witness." Melville looked positively delighted, and Roger was quite sure what would happen now.

When Melville called Eve Franklin as the first witness for the defence, the court was hushed. And the witness did not disappoint. She wore a silk suit of navy blue, which would have been acceptable in any cathedral, but somehow made her figure a thing to marvel at. Her dark hair was a cluster of demure curls. Her face was pale, and she wore little makeup. Her voice was low-pitched, but she was completely self-assured.

She was sworn.

"Now, Miss Franklin," said Melville, "I want you to understand that the court is interested only in your evidence. You must not speak of anything you did not actually see. Do you understand that?"

"Yes."

"You were on Clapham Common on the evening of October the 22nd – or, more accurately, the early morning of October the 23rd?"

"I was."

"Were you alone?"

"Yes."

"Wasn't that rather late for a young woman to be out alone?"

"I'm not *so* young."

Someone tittered.

They're going to believe her, Roger thought, and he felt an even greater tensing of his nerves. Here was a man he knew was guilty, about to get away with it again, unless the police solicitor could throw serious doubt on this girl's evidence.

"I don't think positive accuracy about your age is a matter of great importance to the court," murmured Melville, suavely. "Will you object if I ask you what you were doing at that time?"

"I was walking home," answered Eve.

"I see. There is no public transport at that time of night and you couldn't get a taxi. Is that it?"

"The witness will give us all the relevant information," interrupted the magistrate severely.

"I am sorry, Your Worship. I am anxious only to make this ordeal as bearable as possible for the witness. Why did you walk home, Miss Franklin?"

"Because I couldn't get a taxi."

"Why did you walk across the Common?"

"I often do. Some friends of mine live on the other side of the Common, you see."

"Had you been with these friends that night?"

"Yes."

"What time was it when you left?"

"About one o'clock."

"Can you be more precise?"

"I'm afraid I can't," answered Eve, apologetically.

"Perhaps it is immaterial," conceded Melville. "Did you walk along the sidewalk or along the road?"

"I cut across the Common, on a path."

"Did you see anything coming along the road?"

"I saw a big car," answered Eve. "I don't know what make it was; there wasn't very much light. I know it was a light colour, though – white, I should say. Its headlights were on."

She moistened her lips.

She's lying, Roger thought, desperately, but they'll believe her.

" Go on, please," murmured Melville.

"Just as it turned a bend in the road, a man ran out from the bushes," asserted the girl. She looked as if the moment of horror still affected her, the lying bitch! "He didn't seem to look where he was going, just ran across the road. The car swerved, and I quite thought it would crash. I remember standing still and staring. I couldn't even cry out."

"We quite understand," soothed Melville. "And what happened then?"

"I saw the man fall," said Eve, simply. "He – he simply didn't get up again."

"Did the car stop?"

"It slowed down, then went on."

If she was lying, would she admit a thing which didn't show

21

Raeburn up in a good light, even though it made her testimony seem still more reliable?

"I see," said Melville, quite untroubled. "Now, you saw an accident, one of many sad fatalities which occur on the road, but you did not inform the police. Why was that?"

"I – I was so frightened," answered Eve, uneasily. "I could never stand the sight of blood; it always makes me faint. I just stood staring, not knowing what to do. Then a man came up on a bike – on a bicycle."

"Did you see him?"

"Not very well," said Eve. "He startled me, because I didn't see him at first, his lamp was so dim. He got off his bike and bent over the man in the road. I went a little nearer, and saw he was a policeman. Obviously, there wasn't any need for me, so I hurried away." Her voice was hardly audible.

"You now know that you should have made yourself known, and told this policeman what you saw, don't you?"

"Yes. I – I'm sorry, really. But I was so scared, and I didn't want to become involved with the police."

"I don't think we should blame you for that," murmured Melville, and flicked a glance at Roger. "What time did you arrive home?"

"Just before a quarter to two."

"Do you live with your parents?"

"No, I've a fiat."

"Did you see anyone when you reached the flat?"

"No. No one was up in the other flats as far as I know. I'd a terrible headache, and took some aspirins, and went straight to bed. My head was still awful next morning, and I stayed in bed all day. It was *horrible*! I haven't been really well since, but if I'd known how important it was I – I *would* have come forward, I mean that."

"I'm sure you do," said Melville, glancing at the magistrate. "I have no more questions to ask this witness, Your Worship."

The Police Solicitor made the best of a bad job, but could not shake the girl's evidence.

Two men and a girl were put into the box, and testified that Eve

Franklin had been with them on the night in question until nearly one o'clock, but Melville still wasn't finished.

"Your Worship," he said, after the last witness had left the box, "I would venture now to make a statement which I hope you will agree is timely. It is evident that the accident was quite unavoidable. There remains, however, the charge that my client was drunk and incapable at the wheel of his car. I do not think that was the case. I intend to bring witnesses who will testify to his sobriety not only on that night, but at all times. He himself will tell you that he thought he had avoided the man who ran across the road, and –

Melville poured ridicule on Dr Anstruther Breem's evidence, and even shook the assurance of the mobile police who had found Raeburn near Roehampton.

An hour later, Raeburn was almost mobbed by sycophantic admirers when he left the court.

Roger opened the front door of the Bell Street house, stepped inside, and closed it quietly behind him. He stood still, listening. No sound came from the kitchen. Janet was probably out, and the boys not yet home, although it was nearly six.

He had come straight from Scotland Yard, after a gloomy post mortem with Turnbull and Chatworth. He decided to change into slacks, and turned to the stairs. As he put his foot on the bottom stair, the kitchen door opened, and Janet stepped out.

"Oh! Oh, darling, you scared me."

"Sorry, sweet. Boys not back?"

"They've gone swimming." Janet's quick smile faded when she saw his expression. "He didn't get off?"

"He's as free as the air," said Roger, bitterly. "I'm sick and tired of the whole damned business. The man's so rotten that he stinks. I feel that if I even hear his name mentioned again, I'll throw a fit."

They stood staring at each other, until suddenly he grinned. "Sorry, sweet! No more hysterics. Any hope of an early supper? I didn't get more than a sandwich at lunch."

"I'll have it ready by the time you've changed," promised Janet. "Why don't you have a drink first?"

A whisky-and-soda, sausages, eggs and chips, and a boisterous half hour with the two boys when they came in, damp-haired, bright-eyed, and ravenous, drove gloom away.

At nine o'clock Martin, called 'Scoopy', a massive fourteen, and Richard, called Richard, an average thirteen, came away from television, rubbing their eyes.

Janet said: "Bed now, boys, and don't take all day to get ready."

"No, Mum. I just want to ask Dad something." Scoopy eyed his father, while Richard watched from the door; this was obviously a put-up job, probably schemed to win ten or fifteen minutes' respite from bedtime. "I was reading about that man, Raeburn, who got off, Dad. Didn't you think you'd got him?"

"I did," answered Roger.

"What happened?"

"Either I'm a bad detective, or a witness lied."

"You mean that Eve Franklin?"

"The pretty woman," Richard put in.

"We were reading about it in the evening paper," Scoopy explained. "Do you really think she lied?"

"Between these four walls, yes," Roger said, "but if you breathe a word outside, I'll never confide in you again. Now, off to bed!"

"I jolly well know one thing," declared Richard, his blue eyes looking enormous, "you're *not* a bad detective."

"Come on, Fish, no need to say the obvious," Scoopy said, and dragged his brother off.

Roger slept soundly, woke in a more cheerful mood, and was even prepared for a few knocks in the morning newspapers. Scoopy, five feet ten and absurdly powerful, bounded up the stairs with them, announcing: "You're starred again in the *Cry*, Pop!"

A good photograph of himself stared up at Roger from the morning paper which Raeburn owned, but Roger was interested only in the caption:

CHIEF INSPECTOR WEST, THE YOUNGEST CI AT THE YARD, WHO WAS IN CHARGE OF THE CASE AGAINST MR PAUL RAEBURN.

The case had big headlines, and, as he read, a subheading caught his eye: WASTE OF PUBLIC MONEY.

Richard called out: "Have a game of darts, Scoop? Mum's only just started cooking breakfast."

"Do you more good to check your homework," Scoopy said, but went off.

Roger read on: "Another important factor is the waste of public money. Had the police exerted themselves to find Miss Franklin, a case of such gravity would never have been brought. A man of exemplary character was pilloried in public because of an unavoidable accident. Even the charge of being drunk in control of a car was not established. Mr Raeburn will be a generous man if he does not sue the police for wrongful arrest."

"All right, Mr Ruddy Raeburn," Roger said softly, "if you're not satisfied with getting off, I'll give you plenty to think about."

"The worst of it is you can't answer back," Janet complained, angrily.

"Perhaps I can get Eve Franklin to answer for me," Roger grinned. "If I know Chatworth, this will make him hopping mad. It'd be funny if Raeburn's cooked his goose, after all, wouldn't it?"

"You can have as long as you want to prove that Franklin woman was lying," Chatworth growled. "Concentrate on that. If Raeburn wants to have a fight, let him have it." He glared up, and his shaggy eyebrows made him look ferocious. "You agree?"

"All the way, sir."

"And you've a personal interest, after this smear campaign," Chatworth said. "Concentrate on the job, Roger."

The Yard's attitude was almost identical with Chatworth's. "Get the so-and-so, Handsome, we'll take care of the rest."

Janet said, uneasily: "You make it sound like a crusade, darling." Then she added: "Raeburn's rich *and* clever, that's the worst of it. Be careful!"

CHAPTER IV

EVE

E VE FRANKLIN drew sheer silk stockings over her slim legs, fastened her garters, and stood up in front of the long mirror. She stretched her arms above her head voluptuously, as a cat roused from sleep. She looked at herself with a pensive smile, as if she were practising seduction. When she moved her head, the bright lamp above picked out the lights in her dark hair. Her arms and shoulders were bare.

She sat down on the dressing-table stool, and reached for a cigarette; every movement studied. She lit the cigarette and blew smoke against the mirror, obscuring her reflection. As the smoke cleared, the brightness of her eyes and the sparkle of her teeth showed up through the greyness.

She did not notice the door begin to open, but suddenly a man's face appeared in the mirror – a long, sallow face.

His gaze lingered on *her* shoulders end her body as she swung round in alarm.

"Not bad." He came in and closed the door, then leaned against it. "Going places?"

"I'm – I'm going out," Eve said, sharply. "What are you doing here?"

"Just feasting my eyes," said the man. "You're quite **a** dish, Evie."

"Don't be so crude!"

"Getting refined, are you?" The man slid his right hand into his pocket, drew out a silver cigarette case, flipped it open and lit a cigarette from a lighter fitted into the end of the case. He put the case away before speaking again, and all the time Eve stared at him with an edge of fear. "You don't have to worry, Evie, I'm not going to strangle the life out of you yet."

"Don't talk like that!"

"Well, you expected trouble, didn't you?" He moved forward with a slow movement. He was wearing a brown suit which had padded shoulders, and beautiful straight lines; he was dressed to kill. His oiled black hair swept back from his forehead; there were lines in it, made by the comb. His small lips were rather like a woman's and his eyes were a smoky brown.

When Eve made no comment, he went on softly:

"You didn't think Tony Brown would let you go without making a fight for it, did you?"

Now she spoke, gaspingly: "You – you've no right here! Get out! I don't want –"

"You don't want your Tony any more," interrupted Brown. "I'm all washed up, aren't I? You've cost me plenty, Evie, more than I could afford, and now you've found someone with more money, and you don't even want to say goodbye."

He touched her shoulders. She flinched, but did not try to get away. His long, slender fingers caressed her skin softly, moving nearer and nearer to the slim white neck. He could see a little pulse beating beneath her chin.

He moved his forefinger and touched the pulse, feeling its fluttering.

Eve kept absolutely still, as if petrified.

"Scared to death, aren't you?" the man said.

"I – no! I'm not frightened of *you*." She could hardly get the words out.

"You ought to be," said Brown. He pressed more firmly, his hands right round her neck. "Just think of what I could do to you, Evie. Just think of what Paul Raeburn would say if there were dark

bruises on that lovely neck, if your face was swollen and purple and
–"

"Get away from me!" she screamed, and sprang up, freeing
herself. "Get away!"

"You don't have to worry," Brown repeated. "I didn't come here
to kill you. I'm a fighter, Eve, and I haven't lost yet. I've come to talk
to you. Sit down."

She stood where she was, her hands clutching her throat.

He leaned over, pulled a wrap from a chair and draped it round
her shoulders. Then he pushed her towards **a** divan which was close
to the blue-papered wall. "I said sit down."

She obeyed now, fought to regain her poise, and drew her legs
up, curling them beneath her. Brown pulled up a chair, turned it
round, and sat astride it, leaning on the back as he looked towards
her.

"Eve, you're making a big mistake," he said.

"I know what I'm doing." She was less frightened.

"You don't know a thing, and you're asking for trouble," Brown
said. "Raeburn thinks the police have burned their fingers so much
they they'll stop trying to get him, but they won't. I know the police
better than he does. They mean to get Raeburn sooner or later.
They'll probably find out your evidence was perjury, too, but
whether it happens now or later, one of these days Raeburn is going
down with a hell of a bump. When he goes, he'll drag his friends
with him. He's like that, Evie. He takes you up, but he doesn't stick
to you."

"He'd never let *me* down."

Smoke curled up from Brown's cigarette into his right eye, and
he screwed it up. "Eve, even if you were the only woman in
Raeburn's life, which you aren't, and even if he married you, which
he won't, you'd still be making a mistake, because the police will get
him. But before that, maybe a long time before that, he'll get tired
of you. When he does, he'll know you could go back on your
testimony, and he wouldn't like the risk of being blackmailed."

Eve caught her breath.

"Don't be a fool! I didn't commit perjury. I saw the man –"

"You saw nothing," retorted Brown, and added sharply: "You were with me that night."

"That's a lie!" But she was terrified again.

"It happened so long ago you thought I'd forget," Brown sneered. "Or maybe you told Raeburn's friends that you were alone all evening, so that no one could prove you were lying. Well, someone can. I can. But I know when to keep my mouth shut and when to talk. Right now I'm keeping it shut." Brown paused, and demanded sharply: "How much did he pay you?"

She could not find her voice.

"Whatever it was, you ought to retire on it," Brown said. "A thousand pounds? It wouldn't be less, anyhow. That's a lot of money, and you ought to be satisfied with it. Turn Raeburn in, Eve, and let me look after you. We could go out to Australia –"

He broke off at a new expression in her eyes: repugnance. "So that's the way it is," Brown said, softly. "Okay, Evie, have it your own way, but don't forget one thing: I know you didn't see that man or that car. I know that Raeburn ought to be inside. One of these days, when he gets rough with you, maybe I'll tell the police what I know." He let the cigarette drop from his lips, and trod it into the carpet. "Maybe it won't be so long, either."

He got up, put the chair aside, and tossed a key into her lap, "I won't need that again."

She lay where she was with her legs curled beneath her. Her head was tilted back and her hair touched a cushion behind her. The wrap had fallen off one shoulder. Brown leaned forward and snatched it off, pulled her to him, his fingers biting into her arms. He kissed her with a fury of passion which won no sign of response. Then, as suddenly as he had taken her, he thrust her away. There were red marks on her lips and on her arms.

He turned and went blindly across the room. The tiny hall of the flat was in darkness. He stepped on to the landing, where there was a dim light. He slammed the door behind him.

He stood quite still, his heart thumping, a mist in front of his eyes, and he did not see the man who moved in the hall downstairs. He smoothed down his coat, straightened his tie, and went slowly down the stairs and into the narrow street, near the Thames at Battersea.

The man he had not seen followed him, on the other side of the road.

Brown soon began to walk more quickly, glad of the cold air which made his cheeks sting. He did not notice anyone near him. He walked aimlessly, not caring which way he turned, down this street and that until he reached Battersea Park. The street lighting was poor, but he did not want lights. He walked across a dark, unlit road near the Festival Amusement Park, still and silent, and reached the river.

He was followed all the time by the man whose footsteps made no sound.

At last he slowed down, left the park, and turned into a brightly lit pub. He ordered a whisky-and-soda, tossed it down, and ordered another. By ten o'clock his eyes were glazed and his sallow cheeks tinged with red. He left the pub, and kept reasonably steady as he walked back to the single room where he lived.

Once inside, he kicked off his shoes, tugged off his collar and tie, and dropped on to the bed. He lay in a drunken stupor for some time, and then fell into a deep sleep.

It was a small room with a single bedstead, a wardrobe, a dressing table, two chairs and a few oddments. A gas fire with two broken filaments was near the head of the bed; a slot meter was in the corner.

For half an hour the only sound was Brown's heavy breathing. Then a scratching sound came at the door. Brown slept on. The scratching sound continued for some minutes, then stopped, and the door opened slowly. A little man came in, closed the door behind him, and switched on the light. Brown did not stir. The intruder looked about the room, pushing at the fingers of his thin leather gloves. He went to the gas fire, taking some coins out of his trousers pocket; three shillings were among them. He inserted the shillings into the meter, pausing after each one dropped, and listening in case anyone came up the stairs.

No one came.

He turned on the gas, which made a gentle hissing sound. The smell began to fill the room as the man went out. He made no attempt to lock the door, but crept downstairs, unobserved, and walked off towards the park.

Brown slept on....

Paul Raeburn's Park Lane apartment overlooked Hyde Park, but was high, so that all sound of traffic was muted. There were seven rooms, each luxurious. The *décor* by Lintz was a masterpiece; rich tapestry curtains, rooms in different periods, thick pile carpet everywhere to deaden the sound of movement: this was a millionaire's dream.

In the study, a formal room of carved walnut furniture, leather-bound books and brown hide chairs, a dumpy, middle-aged woman sat at a desk. The desk lamp was on, making crooked shadows of her hand as she wrote in a small book. There was hardly a murmur of sound.

A bell rang, breaking the stillness. She lifted her head and listened, until the maid spoke at the front door.

"Good evening, Mr Warrender."

"Hallo, Maud. Is Mr Raeburn in?"

"No, sir, only Mrs Beesley."

"In the study?"'

"Yes, sir."

"Bring me something to eat in there," said the man.

The woman in the study closed the book and put it away, then turned towards the opening door. Her short, fat figure was wrapped in black silk; there was a deep V at the neck, where white flesh bulged. Middle-aged and plain to a point of ugliness, she had opaque brown eyes and clear pale skin. Whenever she smiled, she showed discoloured, widely spaced teeth; they made the smile seem false.

The man who entered, George Warrender, was short and dapper. He flung a black Homburg hat into a chair and took off his dark overcoat and scarf. Then, pulling down his coat sleeves, he strolled towards the electric fire, rubbing his hands in front of it.

He took one quick glance at the woman. "Hallo, Ma. How are

things?"

"Is it cold out, George?"

"Perishing." He rubbed his hands more briskly. "You don't take much time off," he remarked, and turned his head to look at her.

"I've plenty to do."

"Don't overdo it," advised Warrender. "The way he's going on, we'll have to use our wits again before long. We mustn't take any chances of being tired."

"I think we'll manage," she replied, smoothly.

"Got to," said Warrender. "How about a spot?"

She got up at once, walked heavily to a cabinet, and poured out a whisky-and-soda. He took it, raised his glass to her, and sipped.

They were about the same height, but in bulk Ma Beesley made two of George Warrender, and they were incongruous contrasts in appearance. He was as lean and hard as a whippet. Where her eyes were brown, dark and beady, his were a light grey. Her lips were full and soft, his thin and tightly set. She was ugly; to some women, he would have seemed handsome in a sharp-featured way.

He finished his drink, and said abruptly: "I don't like the way Paul's behaving."

"He won't go too far, George," Ma Beesley seemed quite certain.

"I'm not so sure. He out with Eve again?"

"Yes."

"I told him he was a fool to be seen out with her, but he laughed at me," said Warrender. "The trouble is he's got away with too much. It would have done him good to cool himself inside for a year."

"I almost agree with you," Ma Beesley showed her bad teeth.

"I was almost sorry that we got him off," said Warrender, "but perhaps it was as well. If he keeps going round with Eve, though, there's bound to be talk. He doesn't own every newspaper in the country, and he can't stop all the columnists."

"Aren't you taking it all too seriously?" asked Ma Beesley, easily. "He has plenty of reason to be grateful to her, so why shouldn't he take her around?"

"That's his pet line, but West and Company are bound to think it's fishy."

"They haven't been very bright yet, have they?" Ma murmured. "But be quiet, here's Maud."

Maud, a tall, angular woman in a severe, dark grey dress, came in with a loaded tray containing sandwiches, a Welsh rabbit, and coffee. She put the tray on the desk and went out briskly, closing the door softly behind her.

"No, West and Company haven't exactly shone." Warrender took up the conversation as if there had been no interruption. "But Paul made a mistake when he let that attack go through in the *Cry*. Cops don't like being smacked down. Paul ought to have been all forgiving, and more careful than ever. Instead, he's taken Eve out three times, and had her to dine here twice."

"Well, we can't stop him, and I shouldn't worry too much," Ma Beesley said. "She's an empty-headed little tart, and he'll soon get tired of her."

"I'm not so sure about that," mused Warrender. "She's his type, he's always liked the 38 – 26 – 38 kind. She's quick-witted in some ways, too, even if she is a fool. She might hold him for a long time. I'm not happy about her ex-boy friend, either, Tenby says that he haunts her rooms."

"Well, Tenby's watching him, isn't he?"

Warrender said: "Yes. And if it comes to that, I'm a bit worried about Tenby. He was watching Halliwell for us, and may have seen exactly what happened. Paul seems sure of him, but Tenby's always erratic, and a damned sight too fond of practical jokes." Warrender smiled, almost reluctantly, and Ma Beesley chuckled. "Paul doesn't make many mistakes," Warrender admitted, "but he could ride for a fell like any other big-time man."

"*We* mustn't get too critical, anyhow," said Ma, briskly. "I somehow don't think Paul would like it if we did."

She went to the desk and began to eat a sandwich, making three chins where there had been two, as she munched.

"If you keep eating so much, you'll get fat," said Warrender.

Sitting down by the fire with the tray between them, they ate the

Welsh rabbit, cleared the sandwiches, and were drinking coffee when the telephone bell rang. Ma put down her cup, rose, and stumped towards the desk.

"Hallo," she said, in a deceptively pleasant voice. "Yes ... *Yes*. ... Well, I don't see what *we* can do about it."

From the way she looked straight ahead of her, and from the hardening of her voice, Warrender could tell that she did not like whatever news this was. She rang off, but did not return to her chair immediately. The only sound came from the faint ticking of a clock. Then Ma sighed, walked across, and picked up her coffee.

"I hope you're not right," she said.

"What's up?"

"Paul's at the Silver Kettle with Eve, and Melville has just told me that West is there. That *would* happen, wouldn't it? They both chance on the same place on the same night."

"Chance," echoed Warrender, and he looked very anxious. "That wasn't chance. West wouldn't go to the Silver Kettle, except on business." He stood up. "I'd better go over there. I've got to the point where I daren't trust Paul on his own."

CHAPTER V

ENCOUNTER

THE SILVER KETTLE was large for a night club, and brightly lit. The West Indian band was playing softly, and a dozen couples were jogging rhythmically on the tiny polished floor. Over the head of each member of the band hung a gleaming, glittering silver kettle, five in all. Other kettles hung on brackets on the walls. Here were good taste and luxury without ostentation. The waiters wore tails, the patrons were well-dressed and, at this hour, decorous. In one corner, a party gave promise of things to come, with gusts of shrill laughter.

Roger West in a dinner jacket, and Janet in a wine-red gown with lace over satin, were in another corner. With them was a tall, good-looking man, a year or so younger than Roger, with smooth brown hair, brown eyes which smiled easily, but could also give his whole face a supercilious expression. Now he was smiling, and beating time with a fork.

"Believe it or not, I think you're actually enjoying yourself," he said to Janet. "No policeman's wife should let it be said."

"No policeman should have a friend who's a member," Janet retorted.

"Who called him a friend?" asked Roger, lazily. "I've only known him for twenty years, and half the time he's written books pointing out how the police ought to do their job. So naturally I consulted him about the illustrious Paul Raeburn."

Mark kept a straight face. " Lucky I came back from my lecture in the Americas in time. You're making a pretty fine mess of things. You even suspect dark doings at a respectable club like the Silver Kettle, which is strictly lawful."

"Nothing Raeburn owns is strictly lawful," Roger said.

"I doubt that," responded Mark. "This place is hedged about by rules and regulations, all based on instructions from the police. Five hundred pounds wouldn't buy you a membership if you weren't properly introduced. You two certainly couldn't have got in without my member's ticket. Entering here is lily white,"

"As mud," retorted Roger.

"That's the trouble when you get a bee in your bonnet," Mark complained. "A man must be all black or all white. Raeburn can't afford to be openly associated with anything that isn't properly run, and you know it."

Roger picked up his glass. "Here's to the day when we close the Silver Kettle down." He drank.

"That's sheer vindictiveness."

"I am vindictive," admitted Roger, lazily, but his eyes were hard. "I have a nasty feeling that if he gets too powerful, he'll hurt a lot of people when he falls." He was looking towards the corner where Raeburn and Eve Franklin were sitting. "Given a nice long piece of rope, he'll hang himself."

"When he does, I hope you'll acknowledge your debt to amateur criminologists," said Mark. "What have you discovered about this Eve?"

Roger lit a cigarette and continued to stare at Raeburn's table; Raeburn pretended not to notice.

"She's always looked for the big chance, and seems to have thrown over a faithful boy friend, one Tony Brown.

Turnbull's been checking on him. He's a gambler, racing tipster, Smart Alec and lady-killer, the type you'd rather expect Eve to fancy, always with a few pounds to fling about But he hasn't a chance against Raeburn, and might turn sour on her."

"I'll turn sour on you two, unless someone asks me to dance,"

Janet interpolated.

"My turn!" Mark jumped up.

He was tall and good-looking, and Janet stood out as really something to look at in twenty-three of Roger's hard-earned guineas. Mark was probably now pleading earnestly with Janet to persuade him, Roger, to tell him more about the Raeburn case. It would be worth doing, too. Mark might see an angle which the Yard had missed; it had happened before. He was a serious student of criminology, had written three books which were on the desk or the shelves of any really progressive police office, and he had just returned from twelve months' lecturing in the States, his most popular lecture being: 'Police in the USA and Great Britain: A Comparison.' His hobbies were music and old china, and he had money enough to live as he liked.

Janet looked as if she wanted this dance to go on for a long time.

Roger inspected the people about him. The City and the Mayfair Set were about equally represented in this mixed gathering of the upper crust of commerce and society, an upper crust which remained thick and unyielding in parts. The people present could put up more millions than he could hundreds of pounds; some were fabulously wealthy. One plump old harridan, with a tall, miserable-looking man, was loaded with diamonds; a dozen others carried fortunes on their fingers, at their ears or on their breasts.

Eve Franklin, on the other hand, was wearing little Jewellery. She wore a long-sleeved gown of bottle green, and a green chiffon stole. When Raeburn led her to the floor, her body moved with easy grace, but she seemed to have difficulty in turning her head.

He was a head taller than Eve, very broad-shouldered, particularly distinguished in evening dress. His hair was dark, with a touch of iron grey at the temples; he wore it rather long. He had an unusually striking profile, with a good chin and a high forehead; it was easy to imagine him to be an intellectual. Full face, he was handsome enough; add his money to his looks, and he had everything.

Roger saw a small, dapper man wearing a dark lounge suit come in, nod to the headwaiter, and walk to Raeburn's table. He was noticeable because he was the only man not in evening dress. He walked with his shoulders squared and his back very straight, and was looking towards the crowded dance floor.

It was George Warrender, Raeburn's chief aide in all his activities.

Raeburn spoke to Eve, and they left the floor at once. The band played on, the dancers were circling in a slow waltz; no one else seemed to notice Raeburn.

Warrender glanced towards Roger, and Raeburn did the same. Roger did not look away.

Eve was speaking, and when she finished, Raeburn shook his head. Then Warrender put what seemed to be a restraining hand on Raeburn's shoulder.

Raeburn laughed, shrugged it off, and came towards Roger. He stood by the table as Roger started to get to his feet.

"Don't get up, please," said Raeburn. "I'm very glad to see you here, and sorry I hadn't recognised you before. Are you with friends?"

"With my wife and a friend."

"I'd very much like to meet your wife," said Raeburn. "May I?"

The band had stopped, and couples sauntered back to their tables. Mark and Janet, still on the dance floor, looked across undecidedly, until Roger beckoned.

Whatever she felt, Janet's smile was bright as she came up.

"Darling, Mr Paul Raeburn would like to meet you," Roger said. "My wife ... and Mr Mark Lessing."

"I have heard so much about Chief Inspector West's professional activities," murmured Raeburn. "One forgets that policemen have time to be ordinary family men." The admiration in his eyes was certainly not forced, and his gaze was bold but friendly; he hardly glanced at Mark.

"*Is* Roger so ordinary?" inquired Janet.

Raeburn chuckled. "I don't know him well enough to answer that, Mrs West." He glanced towards the band, which began to play at once, stubbed out his cigarette, and asked: "May I ask your wife to dance, Mr West?"

"By all means."

Janet seemed to hesitate, and then turned away with Raeburn, while in her corner Eve sat like a beautiful image, and Warrender sat stony-faced beside her.

Mark sat down and said: "I think I need a drink."

"Have two, I'm in a generous mood," said Roger. "My chief hope is that he's so swollen with conceit that he'll overreach himself. Warrender knows it, too."

"The chap with Eve, pretending to be happy?"

"Yes," Roger said. "I know him better than I do Raeburn, and he's very clever. He and a woman named Beesley look after Raeburn's private affairs, and a lot more. With Abel Melville, they make a powerful team, and they'll aim high."

"How high?"

"Too high," Roger said. "I'll bet Raeburn's trying to pump Janet, and he's as much chance as I have of getting information out of Warrender or Ma Beesley. If I had to choose between dealing with Warrender or Beesley, I'd take Warrender every time," he added thoughtfully. "Ma's like a great fat slug; you can push as many pins into her as you like and she won't notice." He stood up suddenly. "Sauce for the goose," he said obscurely, and made his way over to Warrender and Eve. He saw a glint of interest, perhaps of nervousness, in her eyes.

Warrender jumped up. "Why, Mr West!" His bright smile failed to hide his alarm. "I didn't expect to see you here."

"I bob up all over the place," Roger said, and his eyes lit up as he turned to the girl. "Hallo, Miss Franklin, I had a feeling we'd meet again." He saw her flinch, and recognised the anxiety in Warrender's eyes. "Would you care to dance?"

"I – oh, I'd love to!" She was overeager to get up, and fear and uncertainty did not affect her dancing; she was like quicksilver, her movements had a natural rhythm, and as she grew bolder, she drew closer. If she gave Raeburn this treatment, it was easy to understand why he liked her around.

"I'm ever so glad we had a chance to meet socially," she said, as the music stopped.

"We never know when we'll meet next, do we?" Roger asked.

She wasn't quite sure how to take that, so she giggled.

Roger took her to her table, where Warrender was all false smiles, then went to find Janet with Raeburn and Mark.

"Your wife is a delightful dancer," Raeburn said, as if he meant it.

"I have luck in some things!"

Raeburn chuckled, and wished them goodnight, all with easy courtesy.

"I trust you didn't bounce off that creature too often," Janet said coldly, when he was out of earshot.

"Only when we turned the corners," Roger said. "Was Raeburn a brilliant conversationalist?"

"I don't know," said Janet. "I talked all about the boys and their examination, and how big Scoopy is, and how Richard thinks you're the best detective on the force. At least he knows I think you're wonderful."

"Did he try to pump you?"

"As a matter of fact, all he really said was that he hoped you wouldn't waste your talents," Janet said, and she was a little uneasy. "I had a feeling that he was really asking me to warn you that if you didn't stop working against him, you'd get hurt. He didn't put it into words, but   "

"I know exactly what you mean," Roger squeezed her hand. "Don't worry, sweet. Mark's on our side now, Warrender is scared, while the little lady was positively jumpy."

"If *she's* a lady—" Janet began.

"How about dancing with your husband for a change?" Roger suggested.

"You are taking Raeburn seriously, aren't you?" Janet asked when they were in bed that night. "I had a feeling that he would try to squash anyone who got in his way."

Roger didn't say: "As he squashed Halliwell," but he knew exactly what she meant.

At nine o'clock on the dot next morning, Roger entered his office. He looked at his laden desk, grinned, rubbed his hands and sat down, glad that no one else had arrived. He opened the files and started running through the cases – all concerned with routine matters.

The visit to the Silver Kettle had given him a bigger fillip than he had realised. Warrender's jumpiness and the girl's unease might be encouraging straws in the wind.

The door opened.

"Morning, Eddie!" greeted Roger.

"What, you 'ere?"

"All fresh for the fray," said Roger. "Why the look of astonishment?"

"Thought you'd be out at Battersea," Eddie said. "Turnbull's over there, 'e asked me to tell you if you came here first. A man named Tony Brown, Eve Franklin's ex, was found dead in his room this morning. Gassed."

"My God!" ejaculated Roger, and grabbed a telephone. "Give me Superintendent Pinkerton of Clapham, quickly, please.... I wonder if Eve knows?... Hallo, Pinky! I've just heard about the Flodden Road job, and I'll be on my way in a few minutes, but there are one or two oddments you could get cracking on before the official report's ready:"

"Always a jump ahead," jeered the Divisional Superintendent. "Tell me what they are, and I'll see what I can do."

"Ta. If you could get me Brown's history, going back to his first tooth, it would help. Then see if he's ever had anything to do with The Daytime, the night club Raeburn owns in Clapham. This could be suicide because of unrequited love, but if it's murder, we might find a double motive."

"Jumping a bit fast, aren't you?"

"I can't jump fast or far enough to get Raeburn," Roger said. "See you at the morgue."

CHAPTER VI

HOW DID BROWN DIE?

TURNBULL, MASSIVE and frowning, watched the pathologist who was examining Tony Brown's body, which was cherry pink except where it had been in contact with the bed. His face was as red as a cherry trodden by a clumsy foot. The smell of gas had now almost gone, although in the corners of the room there were still traces. The tap of the gas fire, the door and the brass rails of the bedstead were covered with a film of grey fingerprint powder, and a detective officer was on his knees in front of the fire, brushing the tap gently with a small camel's-hair brush.

The pathologist straightened up.

"Isn't much more I can do," he said. "He's been dead since late last night. No signs at all of violence. There's the usual pink coloration of the body, and the flesh is flattened where he was lying. He'd been drinking heavily,

I'd say – tell you more about that after the post-mortem. You needn't keep him here any longer."

"Right," said Turnbull.

"Nothing more you want me for?"

"No, thanks."

"All right." The doctor nodded and went out, leaving Turnbull alone with the body and the man who was on his knees. Photographs of the room and the body had already been taken, and an ambulance was waiting outside.

The officer in front of the fire stood up and dusted his knees. "Nothing at all suspicious," he said.

"Sure?" Turnbull was hard-voiced.

"The only prints on the tap are Brown's. I took an impression off his fingers, sir, and they're identical with all the others in the room. He looked after himself; no one else in the house ever came in here. Looks as if he did himself in all right,"

"He may have," conceded Turnbull. "Raeburn might be an honest man, too."

The detective pretended not to have heard. "Shall I send the ambulance men up?"

"Not yet, Symes," Turnbull said. "Have another go at the people across the landing and the woman downstairs. We want to know exactly what time Brown came in last night."

"They all say—" began Symes.

"Try them again," ordered Turnbull, brusquely.

"Right, sir," Symes, who so obviously thought that Brown had committed suicide, turned to the door, which was ajar. It opened wider, and Roger came in.

"Good morning, sir."

"Morning," Roger said, waited until Symes had gone, and said to Turnbull, without rancour:" If you talk to men like that, you'll make them hate your guts, and you'll never get the best out of them."

"Morning, preacher," Turnbull said.

It was a touchy moment. Turnbull, a rank below Roger, was always aggressive, often nearly insolent, as now, for they had clashed before. Roger bit back a sharp retort, and bent over Tony Brown, but soon turned away and looked about him. The telltale evidence of police work was everywhere. He did not ask questions, although, when he looked at the fire and glanced up, Turnbull shook his head. Roger went to the window, overlooking a terrace of grey houses, three stories high, mostly shabby, but some of them resplendent with new paint. At intervals along the street were plane trees, their branches spreading upward, dotted here and there with dry leaves hanging on tenaciously. Three stone steps led up to the front door of each house.

Leaning forward, Roger could see a cluster of trees in Battersea Park; not very far from this spot. Raeburn's victim had been run down.

"Found anything useful?" Roger asked at last.

"Not a thing."

"Know much about this fellow yet?"

"Not much," Turnbull answered. "He didn't do any particular job, but managed to make a fair living. Fond of whisky and women, and" – Turnbull paused deliberately – "in love with Eve Franklin."

"Or just a boy friend?"

"I've talked to one of his friends who lives next door, and I've seen his brother, who lives in Tooting. At one time Brown had a different fancy every few nights, but he's been steady on Eve for some time. His friends thought he was making a mistake. She isn't popular... too expensive." After a pause, Turnbull asked: "Are you going to see her?"

"I am," said Roger.

"Room for me?"

"Why not? But I want another look round here first. What did he have in his pockets?"

Turnbull pointed to a bamboo table on which were a variety of oddments, some taken from the dead man's pockets, and some from drawers in the old-fashioned dressing table. There were two photographs of Eve Franklin, one a snapshot of her dressed in cheap, tawdry clothes; the other a recent studio portrait which showed her as she had looked at the Silver Kettle. There were no letters from her; in fact there was not a letter of any kind, but there were betting slips, several copies of *The Winner,* and other pointers to Brown's habits. Standing in a corner was a saxophone case.

"Wonder if he played that?" Roger picked up the case, and asked casually: "Has the sax been tested for prints?"

"It's so dusty I didn't think it worth while," answered Turnbull.

It would have been easy to say: "Everything's worth trying." Instead, Roger opened the case. The saxophone was bright and shining, as if it had been well tended.

"We'd better find out if he ever played in a band; Eve used to sing with a third-rate dance band, remember." Roger tossed a cigarette stub out of the window. "We certainly shan't get much more from here." He looked up as Symes came back, obviously empty-handed. "Any luck?"

"They all say they didn't hear a thing, sir."

"Keep at it, especially among people who live near by," urged Roger. "Tell the ambulance men to get the body away, and then you stay on duty outside. We want the name and address of anyone who comes to visit Brown, especially of anyone who's already heard that he's dead. All understood?"

"I won't miss anything," Symes promised.

"Handsome," said Turnbull, as they drove back to the Yard, "I've got this Raeburn bug even worse than you. Sorry."

"Forget it."

"Thanks. Where now?"

"I want a word with Gubby Dering," Roger said.

The pathologist was at the large laboratory with several other white-coated men, busy at Bunsen burners, tripods, burettes and evil-smelling liquids, testing bloodstains, oil stains, some pieces of fabric, and – where Dering was concerned – the organs of a dead child.

"Hallo, trouble?" greeted Gubby. "I'm told you've a carbon-monoxide corpus on the way."

"I'd like to find evidence of culpable homicide, too," Roger said.

"Bloodthirsty devil," growled Gubby. "You've got murder on the brain. But you didn't come in to tell me to look for signs of violence. What exactly do you want?"

"Some blood," said Roger.

"Eh?"

"Blood – human blood, preferably, in a small container which I can slip into my waistcoat pocket and open easily."

Gubby looked at Turnbull. "Never follow his example," he

advised. "He's daft."

"My state of mind apart, can you find me what I want?" asked Roger.

"There's some blood we were testing from that arsenic job; we've finished with it," said Gubby. "I can make you a thin glass phial you can break easily enough. Or a small bottle."

"I'll have the phial," said Roger.

Outside, with the phial in his pocket, he looked at Turnbull. "Got the idea?"

Turnbull looked fierce. "No, but let me keep trying. We're going to see Eve, are we?"

"Yes, and we're going to act dumb with her – for a start, anyway. I'm taking that line with all of them."

"Why?"

"I think they'll be eager to underestimate us," answered Roger, quietly. "We've got to make them slip up, somehow."

Billinger Street, where Eve Franklin lived, was only a few minutes away from Brown's apartment. The street was very much the same as Flodden Road, but the houses were larger and most of them had been recently painted. The wind blew straight up the street, and a few dead leaves floated from nearly bare trees.

As the car slowed down, a little man came out of one of the houses and walked away quickly, glancing once or twice behind him.

"He came from her house," Turnbull said quickly.

"Never mind about him," Roger said. "We'd rather see Eve alone, anyhow."

The hall of the house was painted a bright green. A penetrating smell of frying onions came from one of the ground-floor flats, as they studied a notice board, on the wall, on which the names of the tenants appeared in gilt lettering. The sign: MISS EVE FRANKLYN, FLAT 3 had a fresher look than the others. Roger knew that the girl had lived here for only a few weeks; it was a better apartment than her previous one, and was probably part of her reward from Raeburn. It was already established that she had been 'ill' since her arrival, for everyone in the house had told the police so.

The two Yard men walked quietly up the stairs. The door of Flat 4 was ajar, and the whine of a vacuum cleaner came from inside. A shadow darkened the doorway, and a woman with a dust cap on her head looked at them curiously, and then closed the door.

The two men seemed to fill the small landing as Roger rang the bell of Eve's flat.

After a long pause, footsteps sounded inside. Roger rang again. Almost immediately the door was opened, and Eve faced them. She wore a pale, gold-coloured dressing gown, and her hair fell to her shoulders. She stifled a yawn, but her eyes were bright and clear, not those of a woman who had just waked up or was sleepy.

Then she seemed to jump. "What, *you* again?"

"Sorry to have to worry you," Roger began.

"You're not sorry a bit," retorted Eve, "but you'd better come in."

She drew back to let them pass, and Turnbull closed the door. The girl walked into the room immediately in front of her; she seemed to float along, the dressing-gown billowing behind her, slim ankles very white, heels baby pink in gilt mules. The room was a large one, but not expensively furnished. It looked out on back gardens, and another row of houses.

"Well, what is it you want?" demanded Eve. She was keeping her fears in check very well.

"Miss Franklin," Roger said deliberately, "a man named Brown, a Tony Brown, was killed last night. He was a friend of yours."

Eve caught her breath.

"I'm sorry to bring bad news," Roger went on. "When did you last see Mr Brown?"

"Why, last ni—" she began, and broke off. Then, as if realising that she had said too much, she went on:" Only last night, he just looked in to see how I was."

"What time was that?"

"Time? I – I don't know." The shock was beginning to take full effect, and she sat down on an easy chair. "Tony dead – it – it doesn't seem possible!"

"What time did he call? It's important, Miss Franklin."

"It must have been about – about seven, I suppose. I went out at half past, and he – he was here before then. But there must be a mistake. He was all right last night; I've never seen him looking better!" She was talking to cover her increasing agitation, and suddenly burst out: "What do you mean – *killed?*"

"He died in somewhat mysterious circumstances," Roger said ponderously. "We are anxious to find out where he was just before his death, and what was his state of mind –"

"No!" she exclaimed, now almost beside herself. "No, he didn't kill himself because of me. Say, it wasn't suicide, it wasn't! He—"

"Why, had you quarrelled?" Roger flashed.

She stopped, and turned her head away. Tears welled up into her eyes, of shock or grief, it didn't much matter which. When she didn't speak or look up, Roger touched her shoulder.

"Leave me alone!" She brushed his hand away. Her eyes were filled with tears, but they blazed at him. "All you do is to pester me, you and your bloody detectives! It's a lie, that's all, you're lying."

"Don't be silly," said Roger, brusquely. "Brown's dead, and we want to find out why he died"

"I don't know anything about it, I tell you. You've no right to come here and torment me." Eve sprang up, pushed him aside, and rushed towards the door.

She caught them both on the wrong foot, and slammed the door. As Turnbull opened it, Roger saw her rushing into a bedroom across the tiny hall. That door closed, and they heard the key turn in the lock. There was a creaking sound, followed by a brief silence, and another outburst of crying.

"One to her," Turnbull said, "and about ten to you. She'll soon crack. Think she thinks Brown was murdered?"

"I think we might break that door down," Roger mused.

"I'm the rash one of this party," Turnbull said, dryly. "Ought we to take a chance of being rapped for forcing entry?"

"In that hysterical state she might do anything," Roger said, "such as commit suicide! Come on." He put his shoulder to the door, but it did not yield. He took a knife from his pocket, opened a thin blade, inserted it into the lock of the door, and twisted, then pushed.

The door swung open. Eve was lying face downward on a divan bed, quite beside herself with shock.

Roger said: "You'd better get her a drink," and stepped to the dressing table as Turnbull went out. He found a bottle of smelling salts in a top drawer, turned round to the girl and, sitting on the edge of the divan, put one arm about her shoulders, and raised her head. She rested on his arm like a dead weight. He held the smelling salts under her nose, and she must have taken a deep breath involuntarily, for she gasped and sat upright.

Roger got up. When Turnbull came in with a whisky or brandy in a glass, she waved him aside.

"Now pull yourself together," said Roger," we've work to do. Do you know whether Brown had any enemies?"

She was sullen now, as she answered: "No."

"Quite sure?" Roger took out his penknife, casually, opened it, and poked at the quick of his thumbnail.

"Of course I'm sure!"

"Then what are you so worked up about?" demanded Roger. He closed the knife one-handed, and suddenly cried out: "Oh, damn!"

He swung round, shaking his hand. His back was towards Eve when he thrust his hand into his waistcoat pocket, and squeezed the glass phial. Blood covered his hand and streamed up his arm when he turned round.

"Here, we must stop that bleeding," Turnbull said, as if in alarm.

All Eve Franklin said was: "Mind the carpet!"

Roger, holding up his hand, went to a basin, and thrust his hand under the cold water tap.

"Take my handkerchief out," he said to Turnbull.

Eve, who had told the magistrate how she always fainted at the sight of blood, showed no sign of being upset. Turnbull made a professional-looking job of bandaging Roger's finger, as if it were a genuine wound, and was finishing as the front doorbell rang.

"I'll go," said Turnbull. He went into the hall, and Roger peered out to see George Warrender push past Turnbull into the hall.

Ma Beesley lifted the receiver of the private line between the flat and Raeburn's city office, and said: "Yes, who is it?"

"Tell George I want him." It was Raeburn.

"I can't just now," said Ma. "I'm sorry, Paul, but George has gone out. You know that woman who lives across the road from Eve? Tenby dropped her a few pounds to keep an eye on the child –"

Raeburn's voice became sharp. "Well?"

"Well, she told Tenby to say that that handsome man has gone into the flat," said Ma. "The very handsome one, you know. Tenby got away before he arrived, so George thought he'd better get along at once."

When Raeburn did not answer, she went on: "Just in case of any difficulty, I've asked Abel Melville to stand by, but I think it will be all right."

"So Mr Handsome won't take a warning," Raeburn said. "I'll have to deal with him."

CHAPTER VII

MR WARRENDER OBJECTS

EVE SAID: "Who is it?" and stood up, pulling the dressing-gown tight about her waist. Her eyes were swollen and red, and her face was blotchy.

"A friend of yours," Roger said.

"That's right," agreed Warrender, "and Miss Franklyn obviously needs friends. Where is she?"

A hand brushed Roger's arm behind the door.

"Don't let him come in," whispered Eve. *"Don't let him see me like this"* She turned to the dressing table, dropped on to the stool, and began to dab a powder puff into a bowl; heavily scented powder flew up in a cloud.

"Chief Inspector, I insist on being told what has happened." Warrender strode forward.

Roger made no attempt to stop him from entering the bedroom. If the girl did not want to see him, it seemed a good time to let them meet. She was looking over her shoulder, her face covered with powder. Her red-rimmed eyes were staring out of a grotesque white mask.

"My dear Eve," Warrender exclaimed, stepping-forward, "what on earth's the matter? What's distressed you like this?" He put a hand on her shoulder; his voice was gentle and friendly. "Have these men been worrying you?"

"They – yes, they won't go away! I locked the door, but they broke it open. I just can't stand any more of their questioning."

"You certainly won't have to," said Warrender, and his voice became harsh and clipped. "Is this your special form of third degree, Chief Inspector?"

"Don't talk nonsense. We –"

"You appear to have forced your way into this room, and made yourselves objectionable. We shall find out whether it is lawful. Eve, I think you had better stay with friends for a little while. You know the people in Flat 4, don't you?"

"I can't go there like this," she protested.

"Oh, don't worry about makeup." Warrender took her elbow and helped her to her feet. "The police will have no objections to this, I'm sure."

Roger said, stonily: "By advising Miss Franklin not to answer questions, Mr Warrender, you are obstructing us in our work."

"She's in no fit state just now to talk about anything," Warrender retorted, "certainly not until she's seen her lawyer. Come along, my dear."

The woman with the dust cap was now standing on the landing, and exclaimed as Warrender led Eve out: "Why, Eve, aren't you well?"

"I wonder if you will let Miss Franklin rest in your flat for half an hour?" Warrender asked. "The police have upset her badly again."

"So *that's* it." The woman shot Roger and Turnbull a searing glance, and took Eve's arm. "Come along, my dear, come and have a nice cup of tea."

Turnbull whispered: "What *is* this?"

"Warrender is trying to establish the fact that we've been ill-treating the girl," Roger answered as softly. "But let him think he's got us worried. He's got a witness; all he wants now is a reporter from the *Cry!*" He stopped as Warrender came back, and the door of Flat 4 closed on the two women.

"Is it not true that she locked herself in her room and that you forced your way in?" Warrender demanded.

"Yes."

"I shall see that the matter is reported at once. It is outrageous that a young woman should be victimised simply because she has given evidence proving that the police fell down on a job."

"Warrender, you're riding for a fall," Roger said, quietly. "Miss Franklin had a faithful boy friend. That boy friend was with her on the evening when she is supposed to have seen the accident. He was going to make a statement, but he died in mysterious circumstances."

Warrender cried, as if genuinely astonished: "What's that?"

"So you didn't know," sneered Roger. "The one witness needed to prove a case of perjury against Eve Franklin is dead. We can't bring the case – yet. But if Eve and her dead boy friend were out together that night, someone must have seen them. We'll find that someone. Once it's proved that she could not have seen the accident, not all the Abel Melvilles, Ma Beesleys and George Warrenders will keep Raeburn out of jail. And remember this: if you ever stop me or my colleagues from carrying out our duties, I'll detain you and charge you with obstructing the police. The charge would stick." Roger turned to Turnbull. "Inspector, tell Miss Franklin that we're ready to take her to Scotland Yard for questioning."

"You can't do it!" Warrender cried but all his confidence had gone.

"Miss Franklin had the opportunity to make a statement here, and refused," Roger said. "She will now have to come with me to Scotland Yard, and I shall not allow you to be alone with her before we leave."

"Raeburn can break you over this, and he will," Warrender said savagely, and turned and went out of the room.

Eve was sullen, but she dressed and went downstairs to the car with Roger and Turnbull. Warrender was not in sight. The girl got into the back of the car, and Turnbull sat beside her. Roger drove towards the park, taking the long way round along Flodden Road. As they passed Brown's apartment house, the girl glanced at it, then looked straight ahead.

When they reached Scotland Yard, she went up the steps in front of the men. In the doorway she stopped short. The big, round-faced solicitor, Melville, was standing in the hall.

Turnbull whispered; "They moved damned quick."

"Didn't you expect it?" asked Roger.

Melville was smiling expansively.

"Hallo, Miss Franklin, you're in difficulty, I'm told." The solicitor took Eve's hand, and turned to Roger. "What is it you want from my client, Chief Inspector?"

Roger didn't hesitate. "I want a statement from Miss Franklin about her meeting with her friend Tony Brown last evening."

"Well, that shouldn't be difficult. If you ask Miss Franklin nicely, I'm sure she will oblige. Brown was accidentally killed by gas poisoning, wasn't he?"

"You might wait for the result of the inquest before deciding."

"Now, now, Chief Inspector, we needn't get heated about it," protested Melville. "I'm only talking as a friend. Did Brown come to see you last night, Miss Franklin?"

"Yes, but he didn't stay long," Eve said, hurriedly. "He wanted to take me out, but I had another engagement, so I couldn't go." As the words spilled out, Melville's man-in-the-moon smile grew broader. "He didn't like it, and we had a few words, that's all."

A quarter of an hour later, she signed a statement, and flounced out of the Yard.

"Handsome," Turnbull said, when they had gone, "they'll try to take the skin off your back for that. You took a hell of a chance to make the girl crack, but it didn't come off."

"I'm looking forward to the *Cry's* next edition." Roger glanced at his watch, as he spoke dryly. "Do you remember the little man who left Eve's house just before we arrived?".

"You bet I remember him."

"Someone went to warn Warrender, and that little man was the most likely one," Roger said. "Try to get tabs on him, will you? Melville smiled and Warrender blustered, but they were scared in case Eve talked too much."

Turnbull, known as the toughest man at the Yard, said

deliberately; "I'm getting scared because she didn't. Watch your step, Handsome."

For the second time Roger saw his own photograph staring up at him, this time with a caption: THE MAN RESPONSIBLE. The *Cry* had not spared him; the term third degree was freely used, and Eve was built up as a victim of police persecution. It was wholly scurrilous, but one inevitable consequence was that his personal stock would fall.

Next morning, two other newspapers took the same line as the *Cry*. It was difficult to go about the Yard looking as if nothing was the matter, but Roger managed it.

He did not go to the inquest on Tony Brown, at which the verdict was Death by Misadventure. Eve's evidence of Brown's visit made splash headlines in several newspapers. He and Eve, Roger thought ruefully, were sharing press prominence. He checked every incident, everything new and old about Halliwell, his arson and frauds, and his associates; he checked the Raeburn ménage closely; he had every stage of Eve Franklin's life checked, and especially her recent activities. Nothing helped. Deliberately, he kept away from Tony Brown's sister, but he had her watched, and he kept a sergeant at work on Brown's activities.

Turnbull put in every spare minute he could on the case. Mark Lessing studied every report, and spotted nothing new.

Two days after the inquest, Roger was dealing with some routine work when the door was flung open,

"What's all the hurry?" Eddie Day demanded, and when he saw Turnbull, he sniffed. "*Some* people would knock on the door before bursting into a superior's office,"

Turnbull grinned at him as he strode across to Roger, and announced: "We've got a line."

The way Roger's heart pounded told how vitally important this case was to him; it was not only a personal challenge, with his future at stake, but at the back of his mind was fear of the great damage Raeburn was already capable of doing through his newspapers and with his money.

"It's the man we saw coming out of Eve's house when we

called," Turnbull went on. "We've got tabs on him at last. His name's Tenby and he's got a record. How about that?"

"What's he been in for?" Eddie's curiosity overcame his annoyance.

"Counterfeiting, seven years ago. Since then he's been fined a few times for passing betting slips. He was broke until a few months ago, but recently he's started throwing money about, and he's supposed to have a taste for practical jokes. Shall I have a go at him, or will you?"

"Who found him?" asked Roger.

"I've been through twenty thousand photographs in Records, and came across him there," said Turnbull. "The minute I recognised him, I put Symes on to make a few inquiries, and I've just had his report."

"Think Symes can handle this?"

"He's dead from the neck up. I –"

"You and I want to keep out at this stage," Roger said. "We need a good, youngish chap. How about young Peel? "

"He'll do," Turnbull conceded, reluctantly. "Never keen on using him, as his brother's a CI, but you know them well enough to slap the young one down if necessary, don't you?"

"He might not need slapping down," Roger said. "Get him, will you?"

CHAPTER VIII

PEEL v. TENBY

THE LITTLE man named Tenby sat in a corner of the Red Lion, in the Fulham Road, with a whisky-and soda in front of him and a blackened cigarette dangling from his lips. He was red-faced and long-nosed, with a habitually fretful expression. He looked searchingly at the dozen men and women in the saloon bar, rather as if he were sizing each one up.

Detective Officer James Peel stood against the bar, drinking beer from a tankard. He was tall, broad shouldered, and slim-waisted, with narrow hips, and he looked in the pink of condition. His light grey flannel trousers were newly pressed, and his brown tweed sports coat hung open. He laughed easily, showing big white teeth. People were usually attracted to him on sight.

The barmaid was no exception.

"You're not so busy tonight," observed Peel.

"Busy enough," retorted the barmaid. "We've got to keep our eyes open when there are people like you about, you know."

Peel laughed, dutifully.

"Coming again?" she asked.

"I think I will."

A large party came into the saloon bar, as a tankard was put in front of him. He paid for his drink, and moved away to make room for the newcomers. His gaze roamed about the room; he looked at and past Tenby, and then went over and sat near by.

Tenby's bright eyes were turned towards him.

"Good evening," said Peel, civilly.

"Evening," said Tenby. "Better in than out."

"Oh, it's not so bad tonight."

"Bad enough," said Tenby. "Perishing." To Peel's surprise, he took a bag of chocolates from his pocket and popped one into his mouth, then began to sip his drink.

Peel took out a pipe and filled it. There were two other men from the Yard outside, ready to follow Tenby to his room, just off the Fulham Road. Peel had some idea how much depended on his success with this miserable-looking little man. As far as he could judge, Tenby was here simply to drink and enjoy himself. The crowd at the bar came over to the chairs, but there was not room for them all to sit together.

Peel stood up. "Mind if I join you, and make room?" he asked, and sat down by Tenby.

"Mixed crowd," remarked Tenby, gloomily.

"Well, live and let live," said Peel.

"That's all very well, but why don't they?" Tenby's voice was thick, and he did not seem to know what he was saying. "Look at this," he added, and tapped his glass. "Two-an'-a-kick for a bloody nip."

"Got to pay for the peace," said Peel.

"Peace? Who said anything about peace?" Tenby sipped again, and put down a nearly empty glass. "Don't you come the old soldier over me. It's nothing to do with peace *or* war, it's the flicking government. Waste millions, don't they? 'S'awful, that's what I say."

"They ought to economise," agreed Peel, solemnly.

"You're right they should, but take it from me they won't. Civil servants, look at the perishers, running around everywhere. Waste . . . and *paper*. Look at the waste *paper*. A lot less forms and a bit more progress, that's what we want."

"You've never said a truer word."

"'S'right," said Tenby. "I never will, neither."

He turned his head and looked straight at Peel for the first time. Behind his narrowed lids, his small blue eyes were very bright. They seemed to hold no expression, although their directness was completely at variance with his muddled talk and his wet cigarette.

"Have another?" he asked.

"Well –"

"On me this time."

"Well, thanks." This seemed like progress, Peel thought.

Tenby got up and waddled to the bar. He looked tipsy, but he had not been here long, and had made one drink last for over half an hour. Was he following up some hard drinking at home, or was he putting on an act?

He came back with a foaming pewter tankard for Peel, and his own short drink, and dumped them down on the table.

"Never mix me drinks," he said earnestly. "Good rule."

"None better," agreed Peel.

"Talking of the government," Tenby said, "what about the police?"

"Ah."

"That feller West."

"West?"

"'And some, they call him," said Tenby. "Don't you read your papers? Shocking! Wastes a lot o' government money – that's *our* money, chum – an' then he has a go at a girl in her flat. Shocking," he added, shaking his head. "More in that than meets the eye, if you ask me. Ought to be slung out on his neck, that's what."

"You're probably right," agreed Peel.

Tenby leaned forward.

"You'd never believe it," he declared, "but I've been inside."

"*You* have?"

"'S'right. I was framed. And I been fined. Twice. Betting slips. What harm does a bit o' betting do a man, that's what I want to know? The government has premium bonds, ain't they? They've got the pools, ain't they? Tote, too. But they has to pay a lot of big, fat, slab-sided coppers to go about picking on the likes of me for taking a few slips. If I had my way with the police, do you know what I'd do with them?"

"No."

"Drown 'em!" declared Tenby.

Peel chuckled. "A bit drastic, old man."

"Maybe it is," growled Tenby. "But it's painless, that's more than they deserve. The way they treated that girl, and the way they tried to pretend Raeburn was a crook when he's a bit of all right – 'Strewth, I know what I'd do with 'em." He looked straight into Peel's eyes. "Drown 'em," he repeated, and sipped his drink.

"There are some poor coppers about," Peel agreed.

"*Poor!*" Tenby exclaimed. "They get paid, don't they? That's more than some people. I was trying to keep body an' soul together when they nobbled me. Don't mind telling you, mister, I haven't forgotten, and I haven't forgiven them, neither. If I can do them a bit of dirt, that's me – Bert Tenby's the name."

"I can't say I blame you," said Peel.

"I don't care whether you blame me or not," said Tenby. "Why, I'd be hard put to it to keep body and soul together, if it wasn't for a bit o' luck I had."

"Ah," said Peel.

Tenby opened his eyes wide. They looked so innocent, in spite of his manner, that Peel hardly knew what to make of him.

"You struck lucky, did you?"

"Penny pool, nearly five thousand," announced Tenby, "and I didn't pay no tax. A cool five thou'." He gave a slow, childlike smile. "Bit of all right, eh? Do you know what? A rozzer come up to me in the street just afterwards. 'Bert,' he says, 'I want to know where you got your dough from.' 'Dough?' I says. 'Dough,' he says. 'Well,' I says, 'you can bloody well find out, copper.' That's what I said, and walked away from him. Proper mad, he was. More pools and less policemen, that's what I'd like to see."

"Well, it's all a matter of opinion," Peel said.

"So what?" asked Tenby, and ate another chocolate.

Peel could find nothing more to say, and not altogether because he was now sure that this man was toying with him. It was something else, even more worrying. He felt hot – much too hot.

There was a pricking sensation in his hands and feet, and his neck and face were beginning to tingle. He looked at Tenby, whose face seemed to be going round and round. The little bright eyes were staring.

"You okay?" asked Tenby, leaning forward.

"I – I – yes, I'm all right."

"You look bad," said Tenby, interestedly. "Take it easy."

Peel felt that he could not get up from his chair if he were paid for it. The tingling had become a scorching sensation, his face and head seemed to be on fire, and his back and chest were burning. He knew that he was beetroot red, and people were staring at him.

Tenby's voice seemed to come from a long way off. "Sure you're all right?"

Peel did not answer, just stared at him.

Tenby's lips were parted, showing uneven, discoloured teeth in an expression which was more leer than grin; obviously, he was thoroughly enjoying himself. His face seemed to come very close to Peel, and then to recede to an immense distance. The saloon bar was going round now; the murmur of voices was louder in Peel's ears. He tried to sit upright, but could not.

He had been poisoned. He had let Tenby get those drinks; watched him, believing he was doing well, and he had been poisoned.

He tried to think logically and coolly. No one would poison him fatally like that; it wouldn't be safe; if anything happened to him, Tenby would be under suspicion immediately. But there was Tenby grinning like a cat, and the other people staring at him.

The barmaid came across. "Are you feeling okay?" She sounded anxious.

Tenby said smoothly: "He came all over like that just before he finished his drink, he did. Looks bad, don't he?"

"He looks terrible,"

"Better get a doctor," Tenby suggested.

Peel forced himself to shake his head. He was actually feeling better, not right, but better. His arms and legs' seemed more normal, and only his face and head were troubling him.

"He looks a bit less red," remarked Tenby, judicially.

"I'm – I'm all right," insisted Peel. "Don't worry about me."

The barmaid obviously agreed, and went back to serve her customers, while Peel sweated, and Tenby sipped his drink.

"You'll be right as nine pence soon, chum," he declared.

"Yes," muttered Peel. "Thanks." His thoughts were clearer, and one thing was certain: he must get the rest of the beer in the tankard analysed. Tenby's trick could be turned into a boomerang. He stretched out his hand for the glass.

"That's the ticket," said Tenby, "another little drink won't do you any harm. Hair of the old dog, eh?" He giggled. "Lemme help you." He grabbed at the glass, and it fell to the floor.

"Cor strike me!" gasped Tenby. "Look what I've done!"

Peel glared, but did not speak, while Tenby popped another chocolate into his mouth.

Mark Lessing was with Roger and Janet at Bell Street when Peel telephoned his report. A doctor had told him that he had been dosed with nicotine, but had fully recovered. Tenby, the practical joker, had won another round for Raeburn.

But supposing that poison had been lethal?

Was it another, deadlier warning?

Would Raeburn kill again, if he were goaded too far? Would he kill any Yard man who seemed to get too close? Could any man be as ruthless as that?

Only a man who believed that he could really put himself above the law would be. Did Raeburn think he could?

CHAPTER IX

WARRENDER v. RAEBURN

W HEN WARRENDER entered the study of the Park Lane flat,
Raeburn did not look up from his desk. Warrender
walked slowly towards an easy chair and stood by it, watching his
employer closely. Raeburn was reading Ma Beesley's diary of events,
leaning forward, and turning the pages with his right hand. The
movements of his hand were curiously graceful; he was smiling, and
now and again he chuckled to himself; it was a studied poise, and he
had a film-star handsomeness.

Warrender's face was expressionless.

Raeburn seemed determined to keep him waiting. He reached
the last entry, read and reread it, then turned back to an earlier page.
Still Warrender did not move.

At last Raeburn looked up. "Well, George, what are you after?"

"I'm sorry if you're so busy," Warrender said, heavily.

"Must we have sarcasm?"

"If that was sarcasm, we need it. Paul, I work my guts out for
you, and the least you can do is to listen when I give you advice."

"I don't always like your advice."

"It's time you learned to listen to things you don't like,"
Warrender retorted. "And stop grinning at me like a god; you're
made of flesh and blood, and you're not infallible."

Raeburn closed the diary, and stood up.

"I'm glad you admit that I'm human," he said, still smiling. "George, we're both busy men, and we both need relaxation. I take enough, but you don't. Just now I like going about town with Eve Franklin. The girl did me a good turn, and there's no reason in the world why I shouldn't show my, gratitude. You're worrying too much because you work too hard, and your nerves are on edge. Why don't you take a holiday?"

"I was thinking exactly the same thing about you," Warrender retorted.

Raeburn was startled into silence.

"There's no need for you to stay in England," went on Warrender. "You've a dozen good reasons for going abroad. There's enough business in America to keep you busy over there for six months; your interests in South Africa and Australia could do with a personal visit. You could take the girl with you, too, although I doubt if she'd last the voyage."

"George," Raeburn said, "I don't want any more sneers at Eve."

Warrender kept his poker face, but with a great effort.

"Paul, I don't care what you think about it. I'm talking for your own good. I'll tell you again that she's a gold digging little tart whose head's as empty as a drum. No, don't interrupt for once. I wouldn't care a damn if she wasn't dangerous, but the police are watching her, and she'll crack if they keep it up. Get away and let things quieten down a bit."

"One would think we'd suffered a heavy reverse," said Raeburn, unexpectedly mild, "instead of pulling off a big success."

"If you think it's clever to rile the police, you're crazy. West won't let up, and he means to get you. I've just heard from Tenby," Warrender added, abruptly.

"Where does he come into this interesting lecture? Tenby did very well over Brown."

"Well be damned! It was a big mistake to kill Brown; it gave West the opening he was looking for," Warrender declared. "Tenby ought to have reported before taking a chance."

"Now, George, he didn't take a chance worth thinking about." Raeburn was determined to be reasonable. "He saw he could get rid of a dangerous man without serious risk, and I think he was right to take it."

"Well, I don't," said Warrender, flatly. "We could have kept Brown quiet; money will always shut mouths. If we rub out everyone who begins to look dangerous, we shan't last a month. Paul, there's such a thing as overconfidence; we simply can't blot out everyone who might let us down."

Raeburn sat on the edge of the desk, and said:" Perhaps you would be happier with Halliwell alive."

"He had to go," Warrender agreed, "but you were wrong to do it yourself. That was the first thing that worried me. Tenby could have looked after him. If he had, we should have been able to deal with Tenby; we shouldn't have needed to find Eve; Brown wouldn't have been a menace, and you wouldn't be under pressure from the Yard."

"All right, it was a mistake," Raeburn conceded, very slowly.

"Anyone can make one, but now we've got to cover up, instead of leaving ourselves wide open," Warrender said.

"That is where we disagree," responded Raeburn, now his most suave. "George, you will underrate my influence in high places."

"Or you rate it too high."

"You're wrong," Raeburn said, quietly. "We had a brush with the police and had a narrow escape, but that's all. I have powerful friends everywhere and they are making sure that I am shown as a victim of police persecution. Every time West tries to be clever, as with Eve, that will be shown up. The Home Secretary has taken the affair up strongly with the Commissioner at the Yard because West has made too many mistakes. The *Cry* is winning a great deal of sympathy over its persecution campaign, and other newspapers are taking it up. West and the police will soon be so busy getting themselves out of trouble that they won't have time to worry about us."

"You simply don't know West or the Yard," Warrender said, stubbornly.

"You forget that West has to obey orders," Raeburn countered. "He will be told to get on with his job, and stop harassing a highly reputable citizen, such as me!"

Warrender took a step forward, and spread his hands in a kind of pleading.

"Paul, you're starting a vendetta with the police, and I tell you that you're bound to lose," he said. "No friends can help if they prove Eve lied. Why don't you see my point? You've got everything you've ever wanted. Why, ten years ago, you couldn't lay your hands on a thousand pounds; today you're as rich as Rockefeller." When Raeburn didn't answer, Warrender went on desperately. "There must be something eating you. What's behind your attitude, Paul?"

"I want and intend things to happen my way," Raeburn declared. He opened the cabinet and poured out drinks, and when he turned round he was his smiling self. "Don't worry so much, George. Take a week off, and enjoy yourself."

"I don't trust you on your own," Warrender said, flatly. "I daren't go."

"All right, I'll take a week off, too," said Raeburn, briskly. "I've got to make sure you get a break, somehow; you're building this thing up too much. You'll see I'm right when you realise that, in the public eye, I shall figure as a defender of the rights of the people."

Warrender took the drink. "So that's it!"

"That's it," agreed Raeburn.

"You see yourself as a great public figure."

"I do, George! This country's never had a real strong man. Moseley tried, but---" Raeburn broke off. "But we mustn't run before we can walk! Whatever it leads to, I also see you as my right-hand man." Raeburn pressed his shoulder. "When I ran Halliwell down, I did myself more good than I realised. Instead of going to prison, I raised my stock sky-high. I don't want to quarrel with you or Ma, but I'm going to do things my way. You just stand by to pick up the pieces. Drink up, George, and forget it!"

Warrender said, flatly: "I haven't finished telling you about Tenby. He was tailed home tonight. A Yard man was trying to get him to open up in a pub, but Tenby was too quick for him. He dropped a tablet of nicotine into his beer."

Raeburn looked amused.

"I'm getting really fond of Tenby."

"He's got a high opinion of himself," Warrender said. "I don't like men in his position who get ideas."

"So you suggest that we get rid of Tenby now? George, don't let yourself get carried away. If the Yard is showing an interest in Tenby, just send him away for a while. He won't mind a holiday, even if you do."

"You personally can't take a holiday from police attention unless you go abroad," Warrender insisted. "That's what I'm trying to tell you. And I've already told Tenby that if he does anything else without consulting me, there'll be real trouble."

"I'm quite prepared to leave him to you," said Raeburn, carelessly. "Send him some chocolates!" He finished his drink and stifled a yawn. "George, I'm getting tired of this. Let's call it a day."

When Warrender was in his bedroom, undressing, there was a tap at the door. He called: "Come in," and Ma Beesley plodded in. "So it's you," he remarked, glumly. "I wondered where you'd got to."

"Most of the time I was outside the study door," said Ma.

"Think that surprises me?"

Ma gave a little clucking laugh, crossed to the bed and sat down, patting his cheek as she passed him. It was a bleak room with ultra-modern furnishings in black and cream, and against that background Ma looked old fashioned. Her long skirt spread out over the bed; on her plump little ankles were rings of fat caused by shoes that were too tightly laced. She took some pins out of her hair, and two long plaits fell over her shoulders.

"Paul is right about one thing – you worry too much," she observed. "But you're right about another: he must be stopped from going about with Eve."

"What's made you change your mind?"

"Paul has," said Ma Beesley, simply. "He's getting much too fond of her; he isn't just amusing himself any longer. I thought he was, until I saw him after she'd left tonight. *Tcha-tcha!* I'd hoped he'd grown out of that kind of thing. If she gets her claws in too deep, they won't be so easy to pull out."

"How do you propose to stop her?" inquired Warrender.

"I thought we might put her in a compromising situation with another man," cooed Ma Beesley. "I'm sure Paul wouldn't stand for that."

After a long pause, Warrender began to laugh, and to look less worried than he had all evening.

"You old devil!" he said. "Ma, you do me good!"

She gave her little clucking laugh, and patted his cheek again as she passed him.

"Just a minute," Warrender went on, as she reached the door. "Paul said something about going away for a week. D'you know whether he was serious?"

"I've already booked a suite for him and a room for her at the Grand-Royal, Brighton," answered Ma. "He says he wants to be alone." She winked. "We'll let him have this week to enjoy himself, and then we'll look after him." She went out, closing the door softly behind her.

The luxury flat was quiet. All was quiet outside, too; only occasionally did Warrender hear a car change gear. He lay awake, looking at the faint light which shone from the street on to the ceiling. It made the darkness a ghostly grey, and he found no comfort from it. He felt wakeful and restless, and kept going over the talk with Raeburn.

Raeburn's overconfidence worried him, and his overriding ambition worried him even more. Did he really see himself as a kind of dictator? Or the real power behind the political and economic scenes? Was he mad? Or was he simply drunk with success?

The stimulus of Ma Beesley's visit had faded; as always, she had been ready to pour oil on troubled waters, soothing and flattering, so as to make everything run smoothly. Warrender could not be sure that she had meant what she said, was not even positive that she would not tell Raeburn that he was so agitated. He was never sure that he could trust Ma.

Probably no one knew Raeburn as well as she did; she was always at his side, suggesting, prompting, and even influencing his thoughts. Had she the same grandiose dreams? She seldom left the flat, and never failed to appear when Raeburn rang for her. Her attitude never varied, either, and Warrender had never known her to lose her temper. She had worked with them for ten years; only he had served Raeburn longer than that.

All three had worked smoothly together, defrauding elderly widows at small continental resorts, never aiming too high, or attracting the attention of the local police. For who would suspect fat, friendly Ma Beesley of swindling?

The currency problems of the neighbouring countries proved another fruitful source of profit, and Raeburn had begun to spread his wings. He always had the bright ideas. Both at home and abroad, he had turned to property buying, made a fortune, and begun to study the Stock Exchange. Now he controlled a financial empire, was beginning to enter the industrial and commercial spheres, and seldom put a foot wrong.

Then Halliwell had come, as a ghost. In the early days, they had found him in Southampton, managing a successful wholesale business, exactly the type of going concern Raeburn had then wanted to control, for he provisioned many ocean-going ships. Halliwell, easily bribed, had been used to handle smuggled goods, and later to plant a fire bomb on board a sea-going tramp, which was heavily insured at Lloyds. The ship, with a largely fictitious cargo, had sunk.

Afterwards, Halliwell, doing a smaller job, had been caught, convicted, and jailed. Not until he came out of prison had Raeburn realised that Halliwell knew who was behind the organisation.

Warrender had always feared something of the kind. He had been the go-between in the early deals, but had soon employed others, making his own arrangements by telephone, and keeping in the background. Ma Beesley also proved to have a genius for organisation. A few agents caught by the police had been well paid for their silence; the number who knew either Raeburn or Warrender rapidly decreased. So did their criminal activities, for Raeburn now found money making money. There had been rumours about his financial activities until he had bought the *Cry,* and really appeared in the public eye.

They went from success to fabulous success, until a letter had come from Halliwell. Warrender had told Tenby to watch Halliwell, and Tenby had seen Raeburn seize the chance to murder the man.

For years, Tenby, a distant relation of Raeburn, had been used for small jobs, without realising how frequently he had made himself remarkably useful. He had started out as an assistant to a pharmaceutical chemist in the East End, where he had learned a great deal about dispensing and drugs; soon he was practising various forms of crime. For a time he had specialised in doping greyhounds, and had fixed several races for Raeburn in the early days. Humble, willing, and unscrupulous, any unpleasant little job went his way. He was the last direct connection between the days of crime and the days of legal plenty.

After Halliwell's death, he had offered to say that he had been an eye witness and the accident had been unavoidable, but Melville had objected strongly to calling a witness with a police record.

Then Tenby had suggested using Eve Franklin. True, he had warned them that Brown might cause trouble, but no one had dreamed how bad it would be. But to Warrender, the real danger was less in Tenby than in Raeburn's attitude towards him; in his general attitude.

Now he was losing his head over Eve. If Ma was seriously determined to part Raeburn from her, undoubtedly the surest way would be to make him jealous.

Warrender grinned.

He had been lying between waking and sleeping for some time when he heard a faint scratching noise which kept on and on, until he realised that someone was moving in the flat. He eased himself up on one elbow and strained his ears, and the sound kept on.

He sat upright.

The noise was coming from the hall, and he realised that someone was trying to pick a lock.

Only Raeburn locked his door at night.

CHAPTER X

NIGHT ALARM

WARRENDER PUSHED back the clothes and got out of bed The springs creaked faintly, but the scratching noise still went on. He groped for his slippers, straining his ears to catch every sound. He stretched out his hands to put on the light, but withdrew it quickly; a light might show under the door.

He could just make out the shape of the door, and touched the handle. He turned it carefully, in case it should squeak, but it made no sound. He opened the door and saw a faint light in the hall. This came from a torch which stood on a small table and shone on to Raeburn's door. In the light he could see a man's hands working at the lock, and the figure of the map crouching down with his back half turned towards him.

Warrender began to creep forward. There was no need for a weapon, a surprise attack should suffice, for the other was intent upon his task. Three more steps and he would be on him.

He heard a rustle of sound and his heart seemed to turn over. He swung round as a man came at him, and shouted at the top of his voice. He saw the man at the door leap, and felt a blow on the side of his head which sent him reeling towards the wall.

Then a door opened and light streamed into the hall, but Warrender was protecting his face with his upraised arm, and could see nothing. A terrific crack on the elbow made him feel sick, and he dropped to his

JOHN CREASEY

knees.

A shot rang out.

Then a scream pierced the silent darkness which was closing down over his mind, and he collapsed. He did not lose consciousness, but was only vaguely aware of what was going on. There was a confused babble of sound, voices, another shot, scuffling noises, the thumping of feet. He took a deep breath, let it out slowly, and got to his knees. The light dazzled him, but he could see Ma Beesley in the hall. The front door was standing wide open.

Two men were rushing towards it.

Warrender saw a small gun in Ma's hand, and croaked: "Ma, don't! Ma!"

Flame from the gun showed clearly, but the men ran on to the landing, their footsteps echoing. Suddenly Maud appeared, her angular figure framed in a doorway.

Ma Beesley stood in the middle of the hall, wearing a huge white nightgown which made her look like a balloon.

"Ma!" Warrender gasped.

"Lend Mr Warrender a hand, Maud," Ma said, as she crossed to Raeburn's door and tapped on the panel. "It's all right, Paul," she called. "You can come out."

Raeburn had been *hiding* from the danger!

Warrender realised this, as Maud helped him to his feet and into a chair. He was sitting down, his head in his hands, when Raeburn's door opened.

In a blue silk dressing-gown, his hair tousled and his face pale, Raeburn stood staring, for once neither poised or suave. "What the hell's all this? I heard shooting."

"You heard shooting, all right," Ma Beesley agreed. "I wounded one of the pair, too."

"*Wounded?*"

"That's right," Ma said, and held up her gun. "George thought he could be a hero and deal with them with his bare hands, but I didn't take any chances."

"Who – " began Raeburn, hoarsely.

"Thieves," Ma Beesley interrupted quickly. "Just thieves, Paul,

72

there's nothing to worry about. Maud, dear, go and make some coffee, will you?"

The maid went off, closing the kitchen door behind her. Ma stood looking from one man to the other, her fat face wreathed in smiles, as if all this were a huge joke.

"Thieves, I *don't* think," she said. "Someone came after you, Paul. They were trying to get into your room. I have been wondering lately whether you oughtn't to have a bodyguard."

"But who was it?" demanded Raeburn, no longer a great man. "Who would want –?"

"That's one of the things we'll have to find out," said Ma, smoothly. "We'd better stop discussing it now; someone is coming up the stairs. It's another story for the *Cry*, anyway. Paul. Isn't it a pity you can't blame West for it?" She chuckled, and then hurried towards the door, to find a porter in the doorway.

The telephone bell rang in Roger's ears and he stirred, without at first realising what it was. He felt Janet move. The ringing persisted, and almost on the instant he became wide awake. He stretched out his hand, and lifted the receiver from the instrument by the bed.

"What is it?" began Janet, drowsily.

"You go to sleep," said Roger. "Hallo?"

"Hold on, please," came a man's voice.

Roger hitched himself up more comfortably, and glanced at the window. It was still pitch dark, except for a faint glow from a street lamp. The illuminated dial of his watch showed up on the bed table. It was nearly half past three.

Then the night-duty Superintendent at the Yard spoke: "Handsome, there's been a burglary at Raeburn's flat, just been reported. Thought you'd like to know. Here's a chance to look round."

"I'll be there in half an hour," Roger said, very softly. "Do me a favour and call Turnbull, will you?"

Roger was wide awake when he got out of his car outside the block of flats in Park Lane. A policeman told him that the lift was waiting at the ground floor; he hurried inside, and found another constable on duty at the lift.

The front door of the flat was standing open, and light streamed into the passage. A porter was outside, whispering to a third policeman; the Yard DI, who was in charge, had left nothing to chance. Inside the flat, men were talking, and Roger paused in the doorway, looking into the study where Raeburn, Turnbull, Warrender and Ma Beesley were gathered. Turnbull, always a fast worker, lived only a minute's drive from here. On the desk was a silver tray, and the whole group was drinking coffee.

Roger went in. " Good morning," he said, briskly.

Raeburn, standing opposite him, saw him first. There was only hostility in his eyes, but he smiled and raised a hand. "Good morning, Chief Inspector."

Warrender's right eye was puffy and nearly closed up, and his lips were swollen. Ma Beesley, in a blue dressing gown, overflowed from an upright chair, her grey plaits hanging over her huge bosom, her bright little eyes turned towards him.

"What's the trouble?" asked Roger.

Turnbull winked.

"I hope it isn't serious," Raeburn said. "In fact I wouldn't have worried you, Chief Inspector, but the porter thought it necessary to send for the police. I'm sorry you've been brought out in the early hours."

"It's happened before," Roger said, dryly, "Is anything missing?"

Ma Beesley heaved herself up. "You must have some coffee, Mr West. I'll get another cup." She waddled out at once, deliberately leaving the men together.

"Now, let's have it," said Roger.

"We've already told Detective Inspector Turnbull everything," Warrender growled. "Two men broke into the flat. I caught them red-handed, and was attacked while I was trying to detain them. Mrs Beesley got out her gun and frightened them away. Nothing is missing."

"Quite sure?"

"They didn't have time – " began Warrender.

"We can't be positive," Raeburn interpolated, coolly, "but

nothing of importance is missing, you can be sure of that. The fools are probably licking their wounds now."

"Wounds?" Roger was sharp.

"There are some spots of blood outside," Turnbull said. "It looks as if Mrs Beesley wounded one of them. I've taken a quick look round, and there's nothing to suggest that anything's been stolen." Pity, he seemed to add. "I've sent for men from Fingerprints."

"That is quite unnecessary," Warrender was taking this very badly.

"We won't keep you any longer than we have to," Roger said, "but we can't have influential citizens attacked in their homes, can we, Mr Raeburn?"

"How true," cooed Ma Beesley, coming in with another cup. "Isn't it a pity I'm not a better shot?"

"Apparently. May I see your gun?"

"The other inspector has it," said Ma Beesley.

"Have you a licence?"

"Of course I have." Ma was laughing at him openly. "Everything was quite in order, Mr West. I think you will find that the thieves thought the safe was in Mr Raeburn's room, whereas it is in Mr Warrender's. We have to expect such outrages, haven't we? There are so many criminals about, and the police have so much to do." She gave a wide, toothy smile. "Not that they would have found much had they searched every nook and cranny; we keep nothing of value here."

She was saying that the police could turn the flat upside down, and find little which might help to build up a case against Raeburn.

"I see. Excuse us a moment, will you?" Roger said. He went with Turnbull into the hall, where the man from Fingerprints and another detective had started work. "Anything doing?" he asked.

"There are scratches at both doors, but I think the front door was opened with a key," Turnbull answered. "We ought to take the lock down and have a good look at it, to make sure. It could be important."

"If they had a key, where did they get it from?" Roger examined the lock of Raeburn's door, and then glanced into the beautifully furnished bedroom.

"Just made for two, but only one in it tonight," Turnbull said.

"They wore gloves," the Fingerprint man reported, factually. "There isn't a trace of a print."

"A professional job, all right, and with luck it will help to make Raeburn jumpy," Roger said. "What have you started doing outside?" he asked Turnbull.

"I've seen the sergeant on duty on the beat, who's making local inquiries, and I've been on to the office. A copper on his beat saw a car leave about half past two; that was probably the one the burglars came in. Think they were after money?" he asked.

"Don't much care what they were after. If we play our cards right, and show Raeburn that we're going to go to a lot of trouble to catch the burglars, we could get Raeburn and Company on one foot. Warrender's edgy already, and Ma's too slimy. Has she shown you the licence for the gun?"

"It's in order."

"It would be," Roger said. "Right – just worry 'em!" He turned back to the study, where the trio looked rather as if they had been caught in some prank. "It doesn't look as if we're going to get any immediate results, Mr Raeburn," he said. "I'm going to have the lock taken off the front door, to see whether it was opened by a key or a tool – "

"There is no need for that," protested Warrender.

"We must do our job," Roger said, flatly. "We shall put the lock back within twelve hours, I promise you. Meantime, we can put you on a temporary fastening. Mrs Beesley, would you recognise either of the men again?"

"I shouldn't like to say."

"What about you, Mr Warrender?"

"I hardly saw them; just saw one man's hands."

"Since no harm was done, why make such a business of it?" said Raeburn, and now he wasn't even pretending to smile.

Roger beamed. "You can never tell how much harm has been done until you've checked everything, and I'd hate the Yard to be accused of being careless, sir. We might get some surprising results before we've finished, too. Thieves and burglars are like most criminals: they have a long run of success, get overconfident, and then make one little slip, and we get'em. Just like that!" He snapped his fingers. "There are so many criminals about now, as Mrs Beesley reminded me, we can't let these men get away with this."

Raeburn was hard-faced and angry-eyed.

"Anyhow, I think we can safely leave you for tonight," Roger added. "I'll have an officer stationed on the landing, in case the men should try to come back, and have another man in the street. Many thanks for the coffee; it's done me a world of good. Good night." He nodded, and went out.

Turnbull followed him, grinning.

There was a hush in the study after they had gone, broken by a restless movement from Warrender. Then the front door was closed, and silence fell.

"This is the worst thing that could have happened," Warrender said, savagely.

"Don't make too much of it." Outwardly, Raeburn was more himself now. "West's very pleased with himself, but this can't get him anywhere. The important thing is to find out who broke in. I think we'll telephone the *Cry*, George."

The Night Editor, in his office off the newsroom of the *Daily Cry*, sat back in his chair, yawning. The last editions would be on the machines in half an hour's time, and he would be through.

The door opened, and a boy entered bringing him pulls of a new set-up of the front page. He stretched out his hand to take them, and as he did so the telephone rang.

"Put 'em down," he said, and lifted the receiver. "Night Editor . . . Who? . . . Oh, yes, put him through at once." His voice grew sharper and he pressed a bell push. "Yes, Mr Raeburn? . . . *What?*" He grabbed a pencil and began to write.

Five minutes later he rang off. By then the Chief Subeditor was lounging about the desk, a cigarette drooping from his lips, an eyeshade covering his tired eyes.

"Barney, put the UN story on an inside page. We want space for a new one on the front. Raeburn's flat has been burgled, and West's on the job. Build up the story this way: is the Yard wise to give this case to this particular man? Is there a risk of personal antagonism and consequent inefficiency? Then ease off a bit, and be conciliatory. It could be a chance for West to make a comeback, as it should be a, simple job. We look to him to make an early arrest. Got it?"

The Chief Sub-editor said: "Yes. But ----------- "

"There isn't any time to lose."

"This won't take a minute. Sam, how long are we going to keep needling West and the Yard? You're going to build up so that if he doesn't pull the burglars in quickly you'll be able to smack him down hard. I know Raeburn's the owner, but we keep sailing pretty close to the wind."

"You may be right," said the Night Editor, "but write up the story from these notes and make sure we catch the late editions. We can't argue, and it might even give West a break. If he does make an arrest, we'll have to give him a good write-up. One day Raeburn might cut his own throat; but, if he did, where would our jobs be? Better hope he's the winner!"

"I see what you mean," the Sub-editor said.

CHAPTER XI

THE MAN WITH THE INJURED ARM

REPORTS ABOUT car movements between two and three o'clock were reaching the Yard from all parts of the West End and neighbouring districts, when Roger arrived at his office. The chief interest centred on three: a large Austin, a Fiat, and a Hillman Minx, all of which had been seen in Park Lane about the time of the burglary. This was established by half past four. At a quarter to five B Division rang through to report that a Hillman Minx had been found stranded in a side street in Brixton.

"Go over that car with a fine comb," Roger urged.

"We hardly need to," said the Divisional man at the other end of the line. "There's blood on the floor, and blood on the inside of the near-side front door. That means there was a passenger who was probably wounded in the left arm."

Roger's heart leaped. "Nice work! Was the car stolen?"

"We'll tell you as soon as we know."

"Turnbull will come and have a look," Roger said, and grinned when he saw that Turnbull, as lively as by day, was slapping a trilby on to his thick auburn hair.

At half past five, it seemed certain that the Hillman had been stolen from a private car park at a hotel in Tooting. By six o'clock, this was proved. Late in the morning, a man who had seen the Hillman driven off was found. He was a nervous little man who claimed to be a waiter in a Soho restaurant; he had missed the last bus and walked home.

"I was just turning the corner when the car came out of the park," he said. "Nearly knocked me down, it did. I shouted at the driver to be careful."

"Did you see him?" asked Roger.

"Clear as I can see you," the waiter declared. "There's a street lamp on that corner. I'd recognise him again if I saw him. I'm sure of that, but –"

"But what?"

"I don't want to get no one into any trouble," the waiter said, uneasily. "It was only chance that I saw him."

"You won't get anyone into trouble unless they've asked for it," Roger said. "How many people were in the car?"

"Two men."

"Did you see them both clearly?"

"I only got a good dekko at the driver, a little dark bloke, he was. He didn't half give me a nasty look, too,"

"Which way did the car turn?"

"Clapham Road, toward Brixton," asserted the waiter. "It wasn't 'arf moving, too; the road was quite clear. You – er, you won't put me in the box, will you?"

"Not if I can help it," Roger promised.

C Division, which controlled the Tooting area, worked at high pressure, and fragments of information brought in were quickly piece together. The movements of two men seen walking near the car park were checked. Turnbull discovered a policeman on his beat who had seen two men leaving a house in Hill Lane, Tooting, at about one in the morning; they had returned there at about four o'clock."

"Anything definite known about them?" Roger asked.

"We haven't found anything yet," said Turnbull, "but there's one queer thing."

"What's that?"

"One of them is named Brown."

Roger sat back in his chair. Eddie Day, who was making a

pretence of working but was actually listening, exclaimed:
"Crikey!"

"Another Brown, is he?" murmured Roger. "Tony Brown's brother lived out there, remember."

"I remember. Where shall I meet you?" Turnbull asked.

"C Division Headquarters," Roger said.

He was there in half an hour, and Turnbull drove him to the home of Mr Brown. He had already picked up some information about the man. Brown was married, and had just moved into a flat which he and his wife shared with a man called Deaken. Little else was known about him, and it was not even certain that Brown was still at the fiat, which had not been under observation until nearly five o'clock that afternoon. Brown might have left at any time during the day.

A plain-clothes officer from the Division was strolling along the street. He recognised West and saluted, but walked on.

The house was a modern villa, turned into two flats. Roger and Turnbull walked up a short path to the front door which was unlatched; there were two doors inside a tiny hall, and one of them stood open.

A girl of three or four came solemnly towards them, stared, and asked shyly: "Do you want to see my mummy?"

"It's the upstairs flat, sir," said Turnbull.

"Not just now, thanks," said Roger, smiling down, and pressed the bell of the upper flat as the little girl stood watching. A woman called out to her, but she ignored the summons. Roger wished the woman would keep quiet; it was impossible to hear any movement on the stairs.

He rang again.

"Mary, come along in!" A flustered, sharp-faced woman appeared at the door of the ground-floor flat. "I'm sorry she's so disobedient. I simply can't do anything with her."

"I've two boys of my own, so I'm used to children." Roger made himself smile. "Do you know if anyone's in upstairs?"

"Well, I think Mrs Brown is." The woman tidied her hair, and looked at the bell. "I should ring again if I were you; that bell doesn't always work properly. I do hope there isn't anything the matter."

"What makes you think there might be?" asked Roger.

"Well – I think Mr Brown hurt himself last night; he was out late, I know," the woman answered. "And it was quite early this morning when Mrs Brown came downstairs to borrow my first-aid kit. That's right, sir, keep your finger on the bell. Listen." She craned her neck towards the door. "There it is now. I can hear it."

Footsteps on the stairs became audible, too.

The woman showed no inclination to go, and as soon as the door opened she burst out: "Oh, Mrs Brown, this gentleman couldn't make the bell ring, so I told him to keep his finger on it. I do hope Mr Brown is better."

The girl in the doorway said, "Sure, he's all right."

She was a plump little creature with a mop of fair hair, a good figure, and round blue eyes. She looked tired, and the sight of the callers obviously alarmed her. She licked her lips, glancing from Roger to Turnbull, and then asked sharply: "Well, what is it?"

"I'd like to see Mr Brown, please," Roger said.

"He's out." The words seemed to leap from her.

"Then perhaps you can spare me a few minutes, Mrs Brown?"

"Oh, you'd better come in," she said at last, and stood aside, glaring at her neighbour and the child.

Roger and Turnbull stepped inside, and followed her up a flight of narrow stairs which were carpeted in plain green. Mrs Brown walked quickly, and Roger could see the back of her knees and half way up her sturdy, bare thighs, because her linen frock was too short. She had very full calves and ankles which tapered away to small, sandal clad feet. Turnbull made a smacking motion with his big right hand.

"*Is* he in?" asked Roger.

"I've told you: no, he isn't! I wouldn't have let you in, either, if that damned busybody downstairs hadn't been gawking; she never could keep her nose out of our business!" Mrs Brown turned to face them, her lips trembling, her voice hoarse with emotion. Fear? "I can't tell you anything, it's no use asking me!"

"So you know who we are?" asked Roger.

"You aren't the first policemen I've seen."

"I don't suppose we are," Roger said, dryly. "We want to ask your husband a few questions about what he was doing last night."

"I don't know where he was."

"You know what time he got in."

"– was asleep. I'm a heavy sleeper, and I didn't notice. It's no use asking me."

"Three of you share this flat, and the two men were out last night. That's right, isn't it?"

Mrs Brown moistened her lips, and said nothing.

Roger said: "Sit down, Mrs Brown."

She was so nervous that she collapsed into a chair.

Roger glanced about the living-room, pausing to give her a chance to collect herself. Some band instruments, drums, two trombones, and a trumpet in a corner instantly reminded him of the saxophone at Tony Brown's flat. Beyond them were several photographs on the top of a cabinet.

"Does your husband run a dance band, Mrs Brown?"

"Yes," she answered. "Why the hell don't you say what you've come about?"

"You don't want to get your husband into trouble, I know, but it isn't your fault if he has broken the law," Roger said. "If he has, the sooner he admits it and starts afresh, the better for both of you. Where –"

He broke off. He had caught a glimpse of one of the photographs again, and it had put him off balance. Turnbull looked puzzled. Mrs Brown turned to see what had attracted him, as Roger moved past her chair towards the cabinet. There were five photographs, three of men and two of women. Mrs Brown was one of the women; the *dead* Brown was one of the men.

"What the hell are you staring at?" screeched Mrs Brown.

Roger picked up the photograph of the dead man; across one corner was written: "To Katie and Bill from Tony."

"Who is this?" He was very harsh now.

Turnbull had a look that was almost smug.

The woman put out a hand to touch the picture, then drew it

back. Her eyes were brimming over with tears. She brushed them away, sniffed, blew her nose vigorously, and then sat back with her lips set.

"You know damn well who he is," she retorted.

Roger pulled up an easy chair, and sat on the arm. "Mrs Brown," he said quietly, "this is a serious affair, but as far as I know your husband is only on the fringe of it, and hasn't committed any serious crime. He is suspected of having been in enclosed premises last night. A sympathetic magistrate might let him off with three months – and three months isn't very long. Magistrates are usually sympathetic, if we tell them there's reason to be. Don't you think your husband might be better off inside prison than out and about, now that this has happened?"

She was terribly pale. 'What – what do you mean?"

"You know what I mean." Roger took out cigarettes and offered them. She took one, and her fingers were trembling when she leaned forward for a light. "Who is the man in that photograph, Katie?"

"Bill – Bill's brother, Tony," she muttered.

"The man who died in a gas-filled room."

"Died be damned, he was *murdered!* You and the coroner can call it an accident, but he was murdered, do you hear me?" She was fast losing her self-control. "The swine murdered him because he knew too much, that's what happened, and you bloody cops call it an *accident!* It's always the same: just because a man's a millionaire, you don't care a damn what he gets away with, but my Bill – " she broke off.

"Your Bill thinks his brother was murdered," said Roger. "Does he think he knows who murdered him?"

"Raeburn did, of course."

Roger said; "Katie, the police go for their man, whether he's a millionaire or a pauper, but Raeburn couldn't have killed Tony. He was somewhere else during the whole of that evening. Every minute of his time has been accounted for by independent witnesses."

"Anyone with money can buy witnesses."

"This wasn't bought evidence."

"If he didn't do it himself, he paid someone to do it for him," Katie Brown asserted, gruffly.

"If I could get any evidence to prove that, I'd arrest Raeburn at once," Roger said, "but I don't think there is any evidence. Do you?" When she did not answer; he insisted: "Let's have it. Do you seriously think you or anyone else can prove that Raeburn hired a man to kill Tony?"

After a pause, she muttered: "He's too clever for that, but he was behind it all right."

"If Tony Brown was murdered, we're going to find out, and we'll get the man who was behind it," Roger assured her, "but we need all the help we can get. Why should Raeburn or anyone want to murder Tony?"

"Don't you know *that?*"

"I want to know what you know."

"It's all because of that whore he was in love with, that Eve Franklin." Mrs Brown stubbed out her cigarette, stung her fingers on the glowing end, and winced. "Tony made a proper fool of himself over her; he even gave up the band, because she was tired of it. He couldn't see anything wrong in her, the little bitch! If I had my way, I'd tear the skin off her face! All she ever cared about was money. Tony never had a penny for himself when he was with her. Always buying her expensive presents, taking her places, spending money like water on her – and what did he get for it? She dropped him the minute she got her claws into a man who could spend more money on her. If I could lay my hands on her I'd poke her eyes out! Don't talk to me!"

She stopped, gasping for breath. Roger kept quiet, and Turnbull, standing near, picked up the photograph.

"Oh, what's the use?" Mrs Brown went on, in a quieter voice. "I didn't want Bill to do anything about it, but he was always a fool over Tony. He wanted to bash Raeburn's face in, that was all he was going to do; he wasn't going to kill him, he was just going to mark him. There, now you know."

"A lot of people would like to see Raeburn have a thrashing," said Roger. "But why is your husband so sure that Raeburn's behind Tony's death?"

"Listen, copper," said Mrs Brown. "Eve saved Raeburn from going down for a stretch, didn't she? She said she saw the accident, and that Raeburn couldn't help it. That night she was out with Tony, so she *couldn't* have seen it."

Turnbull raised his clasped hands, and shook them vigorously.

"You don't believe me, I know," Mrs Brown said. "You don't really want anything on Raeburn, that's the truth. You just want to put Bill inside; you just want to close his mouth. You damned coppers are all the same."

Roger said: "Why didn't you tell us about this after Raeburn's trial, Katie?"

She bit her lips.

"You knew the case broke down because of false evidence, but you held your tongue," said Roger. "That certainly didn't help us to get Raeburn. Now you talk about him being behind Tony's murder, and say you know Eve Franklin committed perjury, but can you prove either?"

"It's all true! Tony told Bill it was."

"When did he tell him?"

"What's the use of asking all these questions?" she demanded, almost sobbing. "I don't know when he told him, I only know he did."

"Did he tell anyone else?"

"I don't know, but we *all* know it's true."

"Whom do you mean by 'all'?" Roger persisted.

Katie Brown began to talk more calmly. All three people who shared this flat knew what Tony had said, and it was clear that they believed that Tony had been killed to stop him from talking. Katie Brown did not say so, but obviously her husband had some good reason for avoiding the police, and had decided to punish Raeburn himself. One thing shone out clearly in her story: a deep attachment between the two brothers.

Roger let her talk while Turnbull made notes. When she had finished, she sat up, with her plump, shapely legs crossed, and looked at Roger nervously, as if afraid that she had said too much.

"You won't regret any of this," Roger assured her, "but I've got to find your husband, Katie. If Tony was killed because he knew where Eve Franklin was that evening, it's possible that anyone else who knows is also in danger."

She realised that all right, and said stubbornly: "If you think you can get anything from me about where Bill is, you're making a big mistake, because I just don't know. He and Frankie Deaken have gone off for a few days, **but** I don't know where."

"I don't believe you," Roger said flatly.

"I don't care whether you believe me or not, it's the truth," she snapped. "You're only trying to scare me, that's all. There isn't any danger for Bill."

Roger said slowly: "There was danger for Tony."

"Raeburn doesn't know that Bill knows anything!"

"If Raeburn doesn't know already, he'll soon find out that Bill tried to attack him last night. Bill was seen by two people, and the resemblance between the two brothers is so great that they'll soon guess who Bill is." Roger's voice was softly insistent. "I can't force you to tell me where to find him, but you're making a big mistake by keeping silent." "I tell you I don't know!" she cried.

CHAPTER XII

THE BRIGHTON ROAD

THEY COULD get nothing more from Katie Brown, and Roger gave up trying after a quarter of an hour. She was still scared, but not really resentful when they left.

"What now?" demanded Turnbull. "Going to have another go at her, at the Yard, or keep digging?"

"Watch her, and keep digging," said Roger.

One early result of the spadework was the discovery that Raeburn was going to Brighton for a week, staying at the Grand-Royal, and that Eve Franklin would be in the same hotel. Roger promptly telephoned the Brighton police.

"Are you coming down yourself?" asked the Brighton Superintendent.

"Not yet," said Roger. "I'm sending Turnbull and a younger brother of Peel. You know Turnbull, so don't let him get too cocky. I'll leave it to him to get in touch with you."

"Right-ho," said the Brighton man. "We'll help as much as we can."

Roger rang off, not sure whether to be pleased or sorry that Raeburn would be out of London for a few days. At least it would give an opportunity to concentrate on Katie, Bill Brown, and Tenby, but he had a feeling that he ought to find a new angle of approach. Brown was a possible angle, but might be in hiding for weeks, and

Eve was the big chink in Raeburn's armour. How could he widen it?

Months ago he had sent out a general request for information about Warrender, Ma Beesley, and Tenby, and now he took out the files which he checked every day. A report that must have come in that morning was on top of Ma Beesley's file. It was from the *Sûreté Nationale,* typed indifferently, and with several misspellings.

The door opened, and Eddie Day came in.

"Watcher, Handsome!"

"Good afternoon, *Mr* Day," Roger said with exaggerated politeness. "Since when have you been my office boy?"

"'Oo, me? Not on your Nelly! If you mean that Paris report, it blew off the desk, so I put it in Ma Beesley's file for safety. It's about her, ain't it? Says they think she was with a gang of confidence tricksters working the French coast ten years ago, and was married to a Frenchie who died after taking on British nationality. How does that help?"

"It might, later."

"It *might!*" Eddie was magnificently sarcastic. "And one day you *might* tell your pal Lessing that he didn't ought to come straight into the building; he ought to send his name up, like everyone else. I've just seen him talking to Simister."

"Mark is? I wonder what he's after."

"As if you didn't know," Eddie sniffed.

Roger didn't, but word would soon come. He turned back to the Paris report.

Ma Beesley had been suspected of working with two men on confidence rackets in the less fashionable resorts on the Brittany coast. The *Sûreté* had prepared a lengthy dossier on her. After marrying a Frenchman, she had lived in France until 1946, when the whole family had come to England. The husband had become a naturalized Englishman, taking the name of Beesley. There were three children of the marriage, two boys and a girl.

Roger rang through to the shorthand-writers' room, and dictated a telegram to the *Sûreté Nationale:*

PLEASE SUPPLY ALL AVAILABLE INFORMATION AND
DESCRIPTION TWO MEN BELIEVED TO WORK WITH
MRS BEESLEY, THE SUBJECT OF YOUR REPORT
SIGNED BY PIERRE MANNET, INSPECTEUR, MATTER
URGENT.
CHIEF INSPECTOR WEST, NEW SCOTLAND YARD.

He was replacing the receiver when the door opened and Mark
Lessing looked in.

"Spare a minute?" he asked, meekly.

"Just been hired to work here?" Roger inquired. It was wise not
to be too affable, with Eddie Day ready to bristle.

"Don't be difficult," said Mark, dropping into an easy chair. "I've
had a bright idea, Roger. I've just had a word with Pep Morgan who
—"

"If you're going to tell me what a private eye thinks about Paul
Raeburn, I don't want to hear it. Pep's already told me. He once
tagged a woman who was going about with Raeburn and whose
husband was talking about divorce, but Pep was taken off all of a
sudden, which meant that Raeburn probably gave the woman a
mink coat and that the husband was paid for keeping quiet. Pep's a
good divorce chaser, that's all."

"He says that Raeburn was difficult."

"Raeburn's a vain type."

"That's not the point," Mark insisted stubbornly. "Raeburn gave
Pep the impression that he couldn't stand interference with his love
life, and that gave me the bright idea. He's probably as jealous as can
be, and if some handsome, distinguished chap named Lessing, say,
made eyes at Eve Franklin, and Eve has a roving eye, Raeburn might
get jealous. It might even make him do something foolish. I'm told
he's gone to Brighton with Eve," Mark added, airily, "I could do with
some sea breeze."

"Well, well," Roger said, slowly. "It could be an idea, too." He
paused before going on: "I can't stop you going to Brighton if you
want to, but don't forget that Raeburn's seen you."

"Only for a few minutes at the Silver Kettle, when he was much more interested in Janet," Mark argued. "He might fly off the handle if I had any luck with Eve. You want to make him lose his patience, don't you? Or do you like being the victim of cartoons in the *Evening Cry*?"

"What's that?" Eddie exclaimed.

Roger said: "Oh, lor'!"

"Haven't you seen it?" Mark took an early edition of the *Evening Cry* out of his pocket. On the middle page was a cartoon showing three inset pictures of masked men breaking into a house, holding up a car, and at the door of a bank which was broken open. The main picture was of Roger, made to look like an effeminate young man, saying to a motorist: "It is a serious offence to drive when you've had a drink."

"That's 'ot, that is," Eddie said. "The AC will –"

"Never mind what the AC will do," Roger said, more testily than he realised. "Mark, I don't think you ought to dabble in this job. I probably can't stop you. If you go down, make sure Turnbull knows that a Don Juan is about. I don't want to be investigating the murder of Mark Lessing."

"I'm very hard to kill," Mark said.

Brown and Halliwell had probably thought they were hard to kill, too.

Roger found it difficult to concentrate and telephoned Brighton, but Turnbull wasn't there. He left a message, telling him to look out for Mark. He wished he had taken more trouble to stop him from going down to Brighton, although he knew there was little he could do with Mark when he was determined.

If anything should happen to Mark . . .

No reply came from Paris and no other news came in. Mrs Brown's movements were not at all suspicious, and there was no sign of Brown. It was like a case of suspended animation.

Roger wasn't home that night until after seven. The family had supper together, and he was unusually quiet. The boys went up to their room to do homework, and soon there were sounds of thumping on the ceiling, laughter, and then a crash, as if something had been knocked down.

Roger jumped up, strode to the door, and shouted: "Boys!"

There was a moment's pause, before Richard called: "Yes, Dad?"

"You went up there to work. Get on with it. If I hear any more larking about, I'll come up to you."

"Yes, Dad," Richard said, meekly.

"You deaf, Martin?" Roger roared.

"No, Dad, I heard." Scoopy was subdued, too. "Sorry!"

Roger went back to the living-room. Janet did not speak in protest, but he knew exactly what she was thinking: that the case was beginning to get him down. Well, it was, especially now that Mark was involved. It was almost a relief when, at half past ten, the telephone bell rang.

"Oh, let it ring," Janet said. "You can't go out again" tonight."

Roger forced a grin as he lifted the receiver, and said: "West speaking."

"Good evening, sir. This is Sergeant Mallen."

"Yes, Mallen?"

"We've had a report from C Division that, after receiving a visit from a young woman, Mrs Brown left her Tooting flat in a taxi about 9.20 pm, sir. Our man lost the taxi at Hammersmith, but a report's come in that she paid it off near Barnes Common. The driver was picked up on the way back."

"Near the Common?" asked Roger, sharply.

"That's all the driver's told us yet, sir. He's still being questioned."

"I'll come over at once. Send word to Barnes to have the Common watched; we don't want her to slip through our fingers."

"Right, sir!"

Roger put the receiver down, and spoke before Janet could get a word in. "Brown's wife has probably gone to meet her missing William," he said. "Sorry, sweet, I'll have to go."

Janet said, with great deliberation: "Roger, this case has gone all wrong. I hope you know that. It's West *versus* Raeburn, not Raeburn *versus* the Yard. You're taking it far too personally; you really ought to have a rest from it; perhaps you'd see it more clearly then."

"You're probably right," Roger agreed, and squeezed her tightly. "I'll try to ease off a bit, but –"

"You've got to go out just this once," Janet said, and sounded really bitter. "I've heard it all before, remember."

Roger said, quite sharply: "Do you really want me to fall down on the job?"

CHAPTER XIII

IN THE DARKNESS OF THE NIGHT

K ATIE BROWN paid off the driver, and watched the taxi move off. She stood close to the wall of a house, looking about her nervously. A wide, tree-lined street with few lights led to the Common, and the far end was in darkness. She heard footsteps, and drew back into the shadows. A man and woman passed, talking in undertones, quarrelling. She waited until they had gone, then walked toward the Common. Her heart was beating so fast that it almost seemed to suffocate her.

Bill had sent word through an acquaintance, asking her to meet him near the bridge, over the railway on Barnes Common, at ten o'clock. It was now a quarter to ten. She was afraid that someone might have followed her, but no second car had drawn up. The police were not so hot, anyway.

She wished that she had driven in the taxi straight to the bridge; it would have saved her this walk across the dark Common, but she had not wanted to take any chances of leading the police to Bill.

She had put on a pair of rubber-soled shoes which made a soft padding sound. A heavy bag kept knocking against her leg. It was filled with sandwiches, two thermos flasks of coffee, a half bottle of whisky and some cigarettes, soap, and two towels. If Bill was going to be on the run for long he would need all these. She clutched the bag tightly.

She reached the end of the road and paused, peering into the darkness. The main road which ran across the Common was well lit, but it seemed to be a long way off. There was a rumbling sound, and a bus passed, its lights very bright in the darkness.

Should she take this short cut, or walk to the main road where there were the lights all the way? She decided on the short cut.

It might be a good thing for Bill to give himself up, and in any case she was determined to have things out with him and tell him all that West had said. She had spent a lot of time thinking it over, and West might be right. A few months in prison would do Bill little harm, and by the time he was out again the danger might be past.

She was walking on grass now, past clumps of bushes which loomed out of the darkness. Now that she knew that no one had followed her she was happier, although still on edge.

Then she heard voices.

She stopped and peered into the bushes, her heart racing. A man and a girl were talking in undertones, that was all.

She crossed a path, plunged over the next stretch of Common, and over the main road. Further along, the road sloped upward, toward the bridge which carried it over the railway track. The bridge and road were brightly lit, which made the darkness beside the bridge seem even more intense. She reached the spot where Bill had said he would be waiting. Standing close to the wall to make sure that she was not seen, she put down the bag and eased her cramped fingers.

After a while, she whispered: "Bill!"

There was no response.

The silence began to get on her nerves; perhaps Bill had not been able to come, after all; perhaps the police had caught him. Or – *Raeburn*. She wanted desperately to talk to him before he was arrested; he might listen to her. As she tried to pierce the darkness, her body was taut. Cars passed over the bridge, and the beams of their headlights shone within a yard or two of her. It might be wiser to move farther away from the road.

She picked up the bag, and took a few steps into the darkness.

"*Bill!*" she called again.

There was no answer.

She held her watch close to her eyes, but could only just make out the faint whiteness of the dial. It had been a quarter to ten when she had left the taxi, and couldn't be much past ten now. Bill might easily be delayed; she was worrying about nothing; how could he possibly be sure of arriving on time?

She stepped forward, restlessly, then heard someone moving,

She stood stock still.

Yes, someone was moving not far away – she was sure of it; a man was coming. "Bill!" she called, cautiously. There was no answer, but the rustling sound seemed to draw nearer. Why didn't Bill answer? Panic-stricken, she stared toward the sound, and moving forward, she stumbled over the bag.

Perhaps she had imagined those other sounds –

No, there they were.

It might be a dog or a cat. Not a cat, she hoped, she hated cats. It mustn't be a cat! She clasped her hands together, her whole body rigid. Not a cat; no, not a cat!

"Bill!" Her voice was loud now.

The rustling sound was much nearer; it seemed to be all round her, but she could see nothing moving. A car went over the bridge, shedding a bright light above her; if only she had stayed nearer the road; if only –

A hand clutched her throat!

She screamed.

The cry was cut short as fingers pressed against her windpipe. An arm was flung round her, and she was pressed tightly against her assailant. She could not breathe; she began to struggle against that powerful grip, but when she tried to kick out she lost her balance, made the situation worse.

A great darkness was descending on her with that terrible pressure at her throat. They were going to kill her. She was being murdered.

No, no, no!

The pressure relaxed.

She was a shuddering mass of nerves, and would have fallen but for the support of her assailant. She gasped and panted as the air reached her lungs again. She wanted to scream for help, but little sound came.

A voice whispered close to her ear. She caught only the last two words: "Don't worry." She turned and, as she did so, a cloth was dropped over her head and shoulders; she could feel it on her cheeks and chin, piling terror upon terror. She tried to struggle, but it was drawn tightly about her neck. Then she was lifted clear of the ground, and carried off.

Her assailant carried her for what seemed a long distance. She was able to breathe inside the cloth, but swayed on her feet when at last the man set her down. He still held her, and this time she caught his words clearly.

"If you behave yourself, you'll be all right. Don't talk above a whisper." He had a curiously expressionless voice.

"I won't, I won't," she promised, but the cloth seemed to muffle the words.

The cord at her neck was loosened, and the cloth taken off. It was very dark. In the distance were the lights of the main road, just visible between the trees; so she was still on the Common.

"Go straight ahead," the man said, pushing her forward. "Go on, they won't hurt you."

Something clutched at her clothes; she felt her stocking rip and a sharp pain in her leg. She was being pushed through a gap between some bushes. Then the twigs and thorns stopped tugging at her, and she stood free of them with darkness all round her – alone with the man who had nearly throttled her. If only she could scream!

The man said: "I sent that message, your husband didn't. Get that clear. Now answer my questions, and keep your voice low. Understand?"

"Ye – yes."

"You'd better." A hand gripped her arm tightly enough to make her wince.

"Did the police come to see you today?"

"I –" she faltered.

"Did they?" The grip tightened, painfully.

"Yes."

"What did they want?"

"They – wanted – to know where my husband was last night."

"Did you tell them?"

"I didn't know."

"You needn't come that with me! I'm not a rozzer. Did you tell them?"

"No."

"He was on a job, wasn't he?"

"I – I think so."

The man said: "Now listen to me, Katie. I want straight answers. You're here on the Common alone with me, see? I can do what I like with you. Ever read in the papers of a girl being strangled on a lonely bit of common? That'll be you if you're not careful, only you won't read about it. Give it to me straight, or I'll fix you. Your husband was out on a job, wasn't he?"

"Y – yes."

"Raeburn's place?"

"I – I think so."

"What did he want there?"

"He – he doesn't like . . . Raeburn."

"So he doesn't like Raeburn," mimicked the man. "That's too bad. I'll have to tell Mr Raeburn; it ought to keep him awake at night. Why doesn't Mr Brown like Mr Raeburn?"

"He thinks –" Katie began.

Everything came out more lucidly than when she had told it to Roger. The man kept on prompting her, and she needed only a word here and there to keep her talking. The story showed clearly what her husband felt about Raeburn; how sure they both were that Raeburn had been responsible for Tony's death; how clear it was to them that Eve could not have seen the 'accident' on Clapham Common.

Katie was calmer, but no less frightened. It was getting cold, and she kept shivering; now and again her teeth began to chatter, and she could not control them; the man did not try to force her to speak during those spells. He kept very close to her, holding her arm; and, whenever he spoke, she could feel the warmth of his breath on her cheeks, but could not see his face properly; it was just a pale blur in the darkness.

Trees and bushes rustled in the rising wind; there was a frequent hum of traffic on the main road, but all sight of the roadway was cut off from her. There was only the fear and the cold, and this man with the flat, hateful voice.

At last she finished.

"And where's your husband now?" he demanded.

"I don't know!"

"You know as well as I do." The man gripped her arm so roughly that she gasped aloud. He slapped her face with his free hand, and whispered: *"Keep quiet!" She* began to shiver, and could not stop her teeth from chattering. He slapped her again. *"Where is he?"*

"If I knew, I wouldn't be here!"

"Don't give me that. Telling me is your one chance of getting away from here alive. Where is he?"

She felt the savage pressure of his fingers on her arm, his breath on her face. His free hand touched her coat, and began to unfasten the top buttons. His hands were against her warm skin. He put his fingers round her throat, and began to squeeze. This was different from his first attack; this was not just to keep her quiet.

He was going to strangle her; he meant to kill her.

His touch seemed like ice.

"Where is he?" he demanded, between clenched teeth.

"I don't know, I just don't know!"

He squeezed, making her choke, but a scream burst wildly from her lips. She struck out at him blindly, taking him by surprise, so that he loosened his grip. The scream came out, high-pitched, shivering on the night air, a blood-curdling sound. As it welled out, he clutched at her throat again, using both hands now; her cries stopped abruptly; she began to struggle and fight for breath.

Roger pulled up behind a police car stationed on the main road which cut across the Common. A uniformed policeman and a man in plain clothes came up and recognised him, and the policeman drew back. The detective from the Barnes HQ tried to put a note of enthusiasm into his voice.

"Very glad to have your help, Chief Inspector. I'm Detective Inspector Gray."

"I don't know that I can do any more than you," Roger said. "Has anything turned up?"

"Nothing that helps at all," replied the other. "The woman walked down Common Road toward the Common, as far as I can find out, but we haven't found a trace of her since then. She was seen by a couple who passed the end of the road, but none of my men has seen her. We can't search the Common thoroughly on a night like this." He was on the defensive. "We can't even be sure that she's here."

"It's a good meeting place," observed Roger. "Are all the roads covered?"

"Yes, but it's easy enough for anyone to slip through," Gray answered. "I don't want to be pessimistic, but I don't think you've got much chance of finding her – not tonight, anyhow. There are so many ways she can creep out."

"She's probably with her husband," Roger reminded him. "Where does Common Road lead to?"

"This part of the Common only," said Gray, "but once you're off the road, you can turn in so many directions. If anyone had seen her start from here, it might have been easier. I've placed men by the road bridge, and others are searching on either side."

Roger said: "Well, we've got to try." He glanced along the road as a car slowed down. "Who's this?"

"One of our men," said the Barnes inspector. He waited until the driver of the other car came across the road, and Roger saw that he was carrying something in his hand. "Well, what is it, Watson?"

"This *might* be a lead, sir," said the driver. He held up a string bag crammed full of packages. "I haven't examined it closely, but it's a food parcel. There's a half bottle of whisky in it, too. We found it near the bridge over the railway."

"Nice work!" Roger took the bag eagerly, and examined it in the light of the headlamps. The whisky bottle shone, and probably the bag had been packed hurriedly, or the bottle would have been wrapped up. There were two thermos flasks and packages which obviously contained sandwiches; just the kind of things Katie Brown might have brought for her husband.

"What do you make of it?" asked Watson eagerly.

The Barnes inspector said: "Someone might have dropped it during the day, or a couple of lovebirds might have walked off and forgotten it –"

"Forgotten it?" echoed Roger, and his voice was harsh. "With whisky in it? This is almost certainly the woman's bag, too. It looks as if Katie Brown was to meet her husband by appointment, and they were for him. So she wouldn't leave them behind by accident; certainly wouldn't forget to give him the very things he needed. See what I'm getting at?"

Gray said, sharply: "You mean – " and broke off.

"I mean that she was probably waylaid, and might have been attacked. We'll concentrate men on the bridge area – right or left of the road, Watson?"

"The left from here, sir."

"I'll get it laid on," Gray said, at last touched by a sense of urgency.

A few minutes later, Roger pulled into the side of the road near the bridge. Several men were already there, and another car was standing on the bridge itself. More men were on the way. They gathered together by a lamp, and the Barnes inspector gave instructions. They were to take up their positions two hundred yards from the bridge, and then close in on a signal.

"One blast on a whistle will be enough," said Gray.

"Think we ought to make too much noise?" asked Roger. "Let's arrange for the car near the bridge to switch off its headlights, and then flash them three times in succession. How long will the men need to reach their stations?"

"About ten minutes."

"In ten minutes, then."

"Right," Gray said.

The wind was blowing more keenly, and Roger moved about,

stamping his feet. There was a silent spell, when no traffic passed, and the wind dropped momentarily. Roger took out his cigarettes, and was putting one to his lips when he heard a scream.

CHAPTER XIV

THE CORDON MOVES IN

THE SCREAM came from their left; it was impossible to judge the distance. It quivered on the night air, and then stopped abruptly; as it stopped, the headlamps of the car on the bridge were switched on three times in succession, light slicing the darkness.

"My God, you were right," Gray gasped.

"This way!" Watson urged.

They plunged in the direction from which the scream had come, their ears strained to catch another sound, but all they could hear was the padding of their own footsteps and the rustle of the grass. The silence was eerie, even sinister. Roger wanted to race ahead, but forced himself to keep pace with the others. They were about two yards apart, flashing their torches to and fro. Other torches were swinging in all directions.

Bushes loomed up in front of them, and Roger's torchlight shone on a piece of waste paper. Staring toward it, he saw a gap between the bushes.

Watson called out: "Found anything, sir?"

"No. Our bird may be hiding among the bushes," Roger answered.

"Right, sir."

After they had made a few yards' progress, Roger could see why Gray said it was practically impossible to search the Common by night. They would need a hundred men instead of a dozen, and to the Barnes man it must seem almost a waste of time.

Then a man bellowed: *"This way! This way!"*

A dozen torches swung toward the call. Roger saw one beam of light moving rapidly, and caught sight of a man running; he was crouching low, and holding one hand in front of his face.

Watson and the Barnes policeman raced after the fugitive; most of the others turned in the same direction. Roger snatched a moment to think, and then hustled toward the spot where the policeman had shouted; he wanted *to* find Katie Brown. His torch shone through the leafless branches of thick brambles.

The sounds of the chase were growing fainter.

Roger's torch slipped from his hand; hit the ground and went out. He picked it up, and when the light shone out again swung it round. The beam caught a thick clump of bushes ten yards away. He moved slowly toward that. He could see a gap in the bushes; there was room for a man to squeeze through. He stood in the gap, and shone the torch about.

Katie Brown was lying there; skirt rucked up, and still as death.

Roger shouted for help, and then bent down over her. She was unconscious, but still alive.

The man who had attacked her got away.

Katie Brown was able to speak to Roger next morning. There were dark bruises on her neck, and she looked haggard from strain and shock, but she was eager to talk. She shivered when she recounted what had happened, and Roger helped her to make it as brief as possible. Before he left the hospital ward, she promised fervently that if she heard from her husband she would send for the police.

"I really will, this time, I mean that;"

"I'm sure you do," said Roger, dryly.

"Have you – have you found the man?"

"Not yet."

"If only I'd been able to see his face!"

"You heard his voice," Roger said. "Whatever you do, don't forget what it sounded like. One day you might hear it again, and you must be ready to recognise it."

"I – I'll *never* forget that voice." She leaned forward, and touched his hand. "Mr. West –"

"Yes?"

"You haven't got Bill, have you?"

"If we do pick him up before you leave here, I'll bring him along to see you," promised Roger. Suddenly his eyes gleamed, and he rose to go. "Don't worry too much, he'll be all right." He patted her hand, and hurried out.

He drove much faster than usual to the Yard, and reached there just before twelve; with luck he would get Chatworth's approval for a new approach to reach the evening papers. He left the car to be parked by a constable, strode up the steps, and made for the lift.

"Handsome looks more cheerful than he has for weeks," a passing man remarked.

Chatworth was in his office, and was gruff.

"Now what's on your mind?"

"A new line on this job, I think, sir."

"I thought we were supposed to have tried everything."

"All conventional methods, sir; this is offbeat," Roger said. "Why not use newspapers to hit back at him? A lot of them hate his guts. We've plenty to go on, too, and a remark from Katie Brown put the idea into my head, and –"

"You might get some newspapers to run a campaign against anonymous criminals, but they'll never risk libel against Raeburn," Chatworth interrupted, "Still, let's have it."

"The first shot would be in tonight's evening papers; just the full story of the attack on Katie Brown, and the fact that we want to question her husband in connection with the burglary at Raeburn's flat," Roger said. "That will bring Raeburn in smoothly enough."

Chatworth nodded.

"Then tonight or tomorrow morning, we'll produce an angle the press will jump at." Roger felt absolutely sure of himself. "We'll tell them that Katie Brown's condition is serious, and she keeps asking for her husband. We can say that she's terrified in case anything has happened to him, and stress the fact that it's because of what happened to his brother, we can let the press do the rest; they'll ram it home. As Tony Brown was engaged to Eve Franklin, that will bring Raeburn in again. One or more of the papers are certain to run a story about the mystery of the Browns – with a suggestion that they're being persecuted. We've only got to indicate the general line, and they'll jump at it."

Chatworth conceded: "You may be right," and ran a hand over his tanned, bald patch.

"We can't lose anything, and at least we'll make Raeburn uneasy," Roger urged. "We may make him do something silly, and at the same time bring Bill Brown in. I've a feeling that when Brown knows that his wife's in the hospital he'll give himself up, so that he can see her. If the papers say she *wants* to see him –"

"All right," interrupted Chatworth. "See who's in the Press Room now."

Roger was in a better mood at home that night; he had Janet, as well as the boys, laughing.

Not one paper, not even the *Morning Cry,* failed to give the story front-page headlines. Only the *Cry* mentioned that Mr. Paul Raeburn was in Brighton.

There was no word from Turnbull or from Mark, but Roger believed that the next move would be when Brown gave himself up.

Janet was sitting in the living-room that afternoon when the boys came in, unusually solemn. They were helping to get tea ready when Richard, a head shorter than his brother and much younger in some ways, stopped in front of Janet, his eyes looking enormous.

"Mum," he said, earnestly, "you don't think anyone would attack *Dad,* do you?"

"Of course I don't," Janet answered, firmly, but she caught her breath. "What on earth put that absurd idea into your head?"

"Oh, nothing," Richard said, airily, but later, when they were alone, Scoopy whispered: "She *is* afraid of it, Fish."

"Wouldn't it be awful if anything happened to Dad?" Richard breathed.

About that time, Roger was fidgeting because there was no word from Brown, and hoping that Peel was watching Mark closely at Brighton.

The lounge of the Grand-Royal was the show place of a hotel which was a show place of the south coast. It was castle like in its spaciousness. Deep armchairs and sofas, with down-filled cushions, were grouped about small tables which looked too beautiful to be used for glasses, cups, and tankards. Great chandeliers glistened with dozens of small lamps for it had been a dull, cloudy day, and outside it was already getting dark. A deep wine coloured carpet, with a heavy pile, stretched from wall to wall. The furnishings were of dark blue, and burnished copper ornaments adorned the ledge which ran round the half-panelled room.

There were three huge fireplaces, and blazing logs sent flames leaping up the chimneys; the Grand-Royal boasted that it was the best and homiest hotel in England.

Only a few people were there at a quarter to five on that particular evening.

Mark Lessing had a table in a window, and was hidden from Raeburn and Eve by a massive ornamental pillar. By leaning forward, he could see them both. Raeburn's handsome head was resting against the back of his chair; Eve sat on a pouf in front of the fire. The firelight danced on her face and arms and shone through her dark hair, and the mass of curls set off her slender neck and squared shoulders. She wore an exquisite cocktail dress of bottle green, cut daringly low.

Mark doubted whether they were really aware that anyone else was in the room, they were so absorbed in each other. A page boy came in with evening newspapers, and put three on Raeburn's table, without being noticed. Mark beckoned, and bought the *Evening Cry* and the *Star.* He glanced at the headlines, shared between Raeburn and Mrs Brown's fears, and his eyes lit up.

He read the story in both papers, looking from time to time at Raeburn, who had not yet opened his. Then he lit a cigarette, and grinned.

Eve leaned forward, and put a hand on Raeburn's knee; he

immediately covered hers with his. She spoke; he nodded, and Eve got up and walked to the door, knowing she was being watched. Raeburn stood until she was out of the room, studying her swaying hips. When he sat down, stretching out his legs and picking up one of the papers, he was sideways to Mark.

He started at the sight of the first story, and then snatched the other papers.

"Not so good, is it, Paul?" Mark murmured.

Raeburn flung the papers aside, jumped up, looked round, and beckoned a page.

"When Miss Franklin comes back, ask her to wait here for me. I have to make a telephone call."

"Yes, sir."

Raeburn strode off, angry and aggressive. Mark put down his paper and strolled after him. He reached the lift in time to see the doors closing on the financier. He glanced out of the front door, and saw that young Peel was there. He nodded to Peel, turned, and hurried up the stairs. Raeburn's suite was on the second floor, and his door was closed when Mark reached it.

Mark tried the handle, but the door was locked. He heard Raeburn's voice, and by straining his ears he was able to catch a few words; Raeburn was putting in a call to his Park Lane flat. The ting of the telephone sounded clearly when he replaced the receiver, and the sounds which followed suggested that Raeburn was pacing the room. Mark moved away, and tried the doors on either side of Raeburn's suite, but both were locked.

His ears were strained to catch the sound of the telephone bell ringing; yet when he heard it, he jumped. He went back to the door and stood close, heard Raeburn's sharp "Yes," followed by a moment's pause: next, Raeburn said clearly: "George, have you seen the evening papers?"

Mark rubbed his hands.

"I won't have it!" Raeburn almost shouted. "I tell you, I won't have it!.... Whoever is responsible must go at once. . . . Never mind what you've told me, fire him!"

There was another, longer pause. Mark stood, grinning almost fatuously, but before Raeburn spoke again, someone turned into the passage. Mark moved away. A man and woman walked past, and went into a room farther along.

Mark returned to Raeburn's door just in time to hear the ting of the bell, as the receiver was replaced.

He went to the landing, and sank down on to a deep spring sofa, lit a cigarette, and was smoking and leaning back with his eyes half closed when Raeburn came out, obviously still angry. He walked down the stairs. Mark took the lift, and reached the lounge in time to see Eve jump up from her chair to greet Raeburn.

She was startled. "Paul, what's the matter?"

"Get your coat," Raeburn said. "We're going for a drive."

"But, Paul –"

"Get your coat."

His abruptness surprised the girl, but she began to hurry toward the door.

"That's better," thought Mark. "That's much better."

He went outside. Peel came up to him, and asked for a match. As Mark handed him his box, Peel asked: "What did you mean just now, Mr Lessing?"

"Raeburn was annoyed by the evening papers, and I went to see if I could pick anything up."

"Could you?"

"Enough to know that he was upset," grinned Mark. "If you haven't seen the papers, get them – they'll do you good. I'm going for a drive," he added, carelessly, and took the matchbox back. "There's no need to follow me this time."

Peel looked blank. "I am watching Mr Raeburn and the hotel, sir."

"Oh, yes? Then what's Turnbull doing?"

"He's at the station just now - Peel was innocence itself.

Mark's car was parked at the front, Raeburn's in the hotel garage. He guessed that Raeburn would drive toward Hove, and then northward into the country, so he drove slowly in that direction. Raeburn's Silver Wraith passed him, purring along the wide road; Mark's Talbot, making little more noise, followed a hundred yards behind. Now and again, when the Rolls Royce was slowed down by the traffic, Mark could see the couple; they did not appear to be saying much.

The light was fading fast when they turned into the Petworth Road. In the west the afterglow bathed the countryside in soft blue and grey; against the skyline leafless trees stood out, dark and spectral. Hills rose up on both sides, bleak and forbidding. The winding road ahead was dark beyond the beams of the headlights; little white centre marks curved this way and that with the road. All that Mark could see of the man and woman in the Rolls Royce were silhouettes of heads and shoulders.

Eve's head moved slightly toward Raeburn. Mark hardly saw that at first, but took more notice when he saw her nestle against Raeburn's shoulder. Raeburn pulled in to the side of the road and stopped, without troubling to give a signal.

"This is where they make it up," mused Mark. "But they're vulnerable, all right." He drove on, deciding that there was no point in watching them any longer. Raeburn had gone out to try to throw off the effect of the newspaper stories, that was all.

Mark grinned when Peel passed him in a two-seater, pretending not to notice him.

A mile or two farther on, Mark turned a wide corner as a car containing several men passed him, forcing him almost into the hedge. He glared into his mirror at it, and then turned a corner – and his heart jumped.

In the glare of the headlights, he could see a man lying in the road.

CHAPTER XV

OLD TRICK

MARK SWUNG the Talbot's wheel hard over. The right fender brushed against a hedge, and twigs scraped along the side of the car. He drew up, with the rear of the car level with the man, only a couple of feet away. He could not see behind him now, and did not get out immediately.

The man was still lying inert. No other cars were approaching, or he would have been able to see by the light of their headlamps.

He opened the door and got out. *Was* he hurt, or could this be an old trick?

The man was lying on his back, his right arm bent at an odd angle, his left covering his face. Mark went toward him, and bent down. He touched the man's arm gently, and as he did so the "victim" butted his head into Mark's face, and leaped to his feet. It was the old trick, all right, and he had fallen for it. Bitter self-reproach made the situation seem worse. He backed toward the hedge, but before he touched it, his feet were hooked from under him by someone he hadn't seen. He fell heavily.

"Get him over the hedge," a man said, urgently.

Mark felt hands gripping him; he was hauled to his feet. He glanced desperately to the right and left, hoping to see the glow of Peel's headlights, but none appeared. Peel was watching Raeburn; what reason was there to hope he would turn up? Mark was dragged

111

to the hedge; then the big man bent down, gripped his legs below the knees, and hoisted him up.

They were going to toss him over. ... Mark kicked out. He caught the man on the side of the face, which made him lose his grip, and Mark slipped to the ground. The man struck at him savagely, but Mark got to his feet, still on the right side of the hedge. A blow cut his lip, and he could taste the salty blood. He kicked out, making one man squeal and drop away; then, next moment, the whole party was bathed in the glow of headlights.

A powerful car came round the corner and slowed down, its horn howling, and the assailants swung round and. scrambled over the hedge. The end had come so quickly that it seemed unreal. Was Peel the rescuer? Mark leaned against the hedge, gasping, blinking in the dazzling light. He was vaguely aware of two people coming toward him.

"Are you all right?" a man asked, sharply.

This was *Raeburn*: Raeburn and Eve were his rescuers.

"Yes, I'm okay," Mark muttered, and moistened his lips. "Yes, quite all right, thanks."

"You don't look it," declared Raeburn.

"Your face is bleeding!" Eve exclaimed. "What on earth happened?"

"I was held up – by a gang." Put like that, it sounded ridiculous.

"Let's go to the car," said Raeburn, brusquely. He took Mark's arm, and led him to the Rolls. "See what you can do, pet," Raeburn added to Eve, and switched on the light. "I'll move his car on to the right side of the road."

Mark sat on the soft cushions of the Rolls, and had the wit to pull out a handkerchief when Eve took hers from her bag. She dabbed at his lips, which were already puffy and painful. The soft light suited her; her face was only a foot away from him, and her eyes seemed full of concern.

"Close your eyes," she advised. "I can see that the light worries you."

As he closed his eyes, Mark caught a glimpse of Peel's two-seater going by, but Peel did not stop. Eve dabbed gently at Mark's lips and cheeks. He could feel her breath on his cheeks, and was conscious of a curious kind of excitement.

She rested a hand on his knee. . . .

Raeburn spoke from the door: "How is he?"

"I'll be all right," Mark said, and opened his eyes. Eve was a little further away, and Raeburn was looking at him, thoughtfully. A car passed, lighting them up in its headlights. A second car drew up, and the driver called: "Can I help?"

"Only a minor accident," Raeburn said. "You needn't worry, thanks." He waited until the car had gone, then asked Mark: "Do you think you'll be able to drive?"

"Oh, yes."

"I doubt it," Raeburn said. "I'd better take you back to town; you can drive the Rolls Royce home, can't you, Eve?"

Not "pet".

"Of course, darling."

Raeburn handled the smaller car's controls easily. Mark caught an occasional glimpse of the Rolls Royce in a wing mirror, and kept remembering the way Eve had pressed his knee – and the way Raeburn had looked at her.

They seldom travelled at more than forty miles an hour. Raeburn asked questions. Mark made a mystery out of the attack, and Raeburn was appropriately sympathetic. He did not show any sign of recognition, and was affable enough when they reached the Grand-Royal.

Raeburn's suite had three rooms, all furnished in the ultra-luxurious style of the Grand-Royal. The main bedroom was his; a smaller one was reserved in case Warrender or Mrs Beesley needed to spend a night there.

Eve's room was on the next floor up.

When Raeburn arrived, Eve rose from an easy chair in the hall. "How is he?"

"You ought to know," Raeburn said, sharply, "you were close enough to him." He stood in front of her, eyes hard, body rigid. "I didn't tell you to seduce the man."

"Paul!"

Raeburn said: "Eve, if you ever double-cross me, I'll break you. Understand that?"

"I don't understand you," she protested, almost tearfully. "I can't make out what's happened to you. I only dabbed at his face; he was in a really bad way."

"I was watching," Raeburn said. "I didn't like what I saw."

"You're crazy to be jealous of a man I've never seen before! I was only trying to help him because you asked me to." Eve sounded really distressed, but a hardness in her eyes did not match the note in her voice. "Don't be unreasonable, darling."

"You have seen him before," said Raeburn. "He was at the Silver Kettle with West that night. You know what I feel about West."

Eve was shocked into silence.

Raeburn stepped past her, and lit a cigarette. He turned on his heel, and looked at her again, letting the smoke trickle from his nostrils.

She went near him. "Paul! I'd no idea."

"Oh, I'm not blaming you for who he is," Raeburn said, with studied carelessness. "I just didn't like the way you behaved with him. Whenever you get near a good looking man, you revert to nature. I've seen it happen before. If you know what's good for you, you'll give up those old habits."

"I have to be civil," Eve protested.

"That's right; just be civil."

"I simply *can't* understand you," Eve protested, in a sharper voice. "Ever since tea, you've been a different man. Has anything happened? Has anything gone wrong?"

Raeburn said: "Yes, but it needn't worry you. You behave yourself, and leave the rest to me, and keep away from other men, or I'll –"

A swift change in Eve's expression stopped him; he had never seen her angry before, but she was angry now.

"You don't *own* me, remember. Or do you think you do? Why not just lock me up in a room, and come and pet me whenever you feel in the mood?"

114

Raeburn said, slowly: "So *that's* how you feel."

"It's how you're making me feel."

"That's a different tale of affection from any I've heard before," Raeburn said. "There are two sides to little Eve." He sneered at her. "You aren't making the mistake of thinking that because you saved me from prison you can be temperamental, are you? You're a common little piece with the right shape, but I could –"

She slapped his face.

Raeburn staggered back, and for an instant looked as if he could kill her. But suddenly she flung herself forward, her arms about him, pressing her body against him, kissing him with a passion which was almost terrible to see.

The look in his eyes changed, too. He thrust her away from him, and held her at arm's length; in her passion, her beauty was the beauty of fire.

"You're mine, do you understand?" he said, chokingly. "I'll kill any other man who touches you."

Eve was lying back, with her head resting on a cushion. Her hair was loose about her shoulders; her slim legs were drawn up under her. Raeburn was sitting at the other end of the sofa, quite rational now.

"When I recognised this stranger on the road as the man who was with West, at the Silver Kettle, I could have run him over," he said, and neither of them seemed to think of Halliwell. "Warrender had told me that a friend of West's was staying here, and had promised to deal with him."

"How can he deal with anyone?" asked Eve, lazily.

Raeburn laughed.

"What's funny about that?" She pouted.

"You're much funnier than you realise, sometimes," said Raeburn, "but it's a good thing you're not clever."

Eve made a face, but something Tony Brown had said sprang to her mind. She wasn't 'clever'. Tony had said that, in the long run, Raeburn would spurn her for a clever woman. Perhaps she was cleverer than men knew.

Raeburn went on: "Warrender had laid everything on all right; we interrupted the party he'd arranged. I hope Lessing sees the funny side of that, too."

Eve swung her legs down, and got up.

"Somehow, I think he will," she said. "Sweetie, I think I ought to go and dress for dinner."

When she had gone, Raeburn poured himself out a whisky-and-soda, and drank it while standing before the fireplace and looking moodily at the flames. Eve already knew a great deal which could be very dangerous. She had probably guessed the truth about the road incident, and there had been no point in refusing to talk about it, but he would have to be very careful with her. Warrender had been right about that.

He finished his drink, helped himself to another, and had nearly finished it when there was a tap at the door.

"Come in," he called.

Warrender entered.

CHAPTER XVI

WARRENDER PROPOSES

RAEBURN DID not try to hide his surprise. Warrender gave a thin-lipped smile, and walked to the cabinet. He poured himself a drink, before taking off his coat and flinging it over a chair. He dropped his hat, scarf, and gloves into the chair, each movement deliberate and calculated.

"Well, Paul," he said, at last. "Here's luck!"

"Do we need luck?" Raeburn asked.

"I'm beginning to think so," said Warrender.

"So you're still a prophet of gloom. Why didn't you leave me alone for a week, George?"

"Things have altered somewhat," Warrender said, flatly. "You thought so when you telephoned, didn't you?

There are a lot of things one can't say over the telephone. I thought you might like a cosy little talk."

Raeburn said: "Provided it doesn't take too long. I'm due for dinner at half past seven."

"And it's now half past six," said Warrender. He tossed down his drink. "Paul, this time I know I'm right. Those newspaper stories haven't done us any good, and they're only the beginning. Chatworth told the Press plenty today. He's managed to make them draw a line between you and Tony Brown's death, with Bill Brown's disappearance and last night's attack on Katie Brown. It was very clever. There are no grounds for a libel action; Abel says there isn't a thing you can do. He also says you'd be a fool if you tried."

Raeburn did not speak.

"I don't know how far West is behind this," Warrender said, "but I think he's the main cause of the trouble. He's certainly responsible for Mark Lessing being down here. There are two men from Scotland Yard here as well. Unless we do something drastic, we'll let ourselves be driven into a corner."

Raeburn said, slowly. "It's your job to keep me out of corners."

"I can't unless you help."

"Can you, anyway? Why didn't you make sure that I wasn't at hand when Lessing was attacked?"

"I didn't arrange that," Warrender said, sourly. "Tenby told me he was fixing something – and apparently he chose to do it that way. You're the one who likes Tenby's little tricks. From the time you let him get away with Brown's murder, he's been a menace. He was told to get information out of Katie Brown, not to attempt to murder her. I've tried to get in touch with him since, but he's lying low. I haven't heard whether the girl did give anything away, or even whether she knows anything."

Raeburn said: "You ought to know yourself."

"I can't go all over London looking for Tenby," retorted Warrender, "and just now I'm keeping in the background. How did you know about the attack on Lessing?"

"I picked him up after it was over."

"Oh, God!" Warrender gave a twisted smile. "Well, that ought to appeal to Tenby's sense of humour. But he's using hired men at Barnes and down here, while he's been sitting pretty, eating his blasted chocolates. I tell you, he's got too big for his boots, and he knows a damned sight too much."

"What will it take to buy him off?" Raeburn asked.

"I don't know," Warrender answered. "I don't even know whether he can be bought." He smoothed down his oily hair, and hesitated before going on: "Then there's Eve – and don't jump down my throat just because I mention her name. She knows a sight too much for my peace of mind. She nearly cracked when West called on her."

"That was because he told her about Brown," Raeburn defended her.

"All the same, if I hadn't arrived, she might have told the lot," Warrender said. "The police are watching her all the time, and if West ever got tough with her, she'd talk. Paul, Ma and I have been working on this problem most of the day. It's a big one, and you've got to face it. The only way to make sure you're safe is to get rid of Tenby *and* Eve. They're witnesses who could damn you, and it's no use pretending they're not dangerous."

It was a long time before Raeburn spoke. Then he said very tensely: "If that's the way it has to be, that's the way it will be."

Warrender moved slowly to a chair, and sat down. He did not smile, but the tension had gone from his manner. He smoothed his hair again, finished his drink, and put the glass on the floor by his side.

"That's more like it," he said.

"But nothing is to be done without consulting me," Raeburn ordered, sharply.

"It won't be, Paul. This is the way I see it," Warrender went on, smoothly. "Tenby can prove you ran Halliwell down deliberately, and as we can't pin much on Tenby, he's got the upper hand. Eve would have to admit to perjury, but she might, if the pressure was hard enough. Right?"

"Yes."

"We could put them both away, and have West and the Yard after us every minute of the day – or we could be more cunning, Paul."

"How?"

"Kill Eve, and frame Tenby for it, so that Tenby would know he hadn't a chance, once the police got him. His one hope would be to get out of the country," Warrender went on. "So we'd fix his passport and his passage, and he'd never dare open his mouth."

He stopped, stood up, and poured himself another drink.

"Can you fix it?" Raeburn asked, abruptly.

"Yes."

"Who are you going to use?"

"I'm not using anyone any more. I'll do it myself," Warrender said, very steadily. "That way, it's safe, and there'll be no one left to talk."

There was a long pause, then:

"When?" asked Raeburn.

"Soon. You'd better be recalled to London tomorrow or the next day," Warrender answered. "Paul, I know you hate this like hell, but we can't avoid it, and there are plenty more floozies. The police won't let up until they've got someone, and the truth about Eve's evidence is bound to come out. You'll be safe if we can fix it all on Tenby. You won't back down?" He was anxious.

"I won't back down," promised Raeburn.

In spite of his swollen face and tender lips, Mark went in to dinner that night. His table was some distance away from Raeburn's, but he could see the couple clearly. Eve was wearing a royal blue gown, backless and almost frontless. Raeburn was in a dinner jacket. They were drinking champagne; whatever had passed between them during the afternoon, peace was quite restored. Eve appeared to be almost deliriously happy, and Raeburn was being the real gallant.

"So it *is* love," Mark marvelled.

Fog had descended on London during the night, and the newspapers had not arrived by the time Roger was ready to leave for the Yard, next day. The boys had left early, and Janet called anxiously from the kitchen door: "I think it's getting worse."

"I'll take it slowly," Roger reassured her.

It was a trying drive, but when he reached the Yard a pile of newspapers was on his desk. The story of the 'badly injured' woman in hospital, asking to see her husband, must now be known in nearly every household in the country; and, in each story, Raeburn's name was mentioned. Pictures of Eve were in several papers, and two had photographs of Tony Brown.

There was a cheerful note from Mark, and details of the attack from Turnbull who had added a note: *'Looks like R. is getting desperate, and we're worrying him.'*

120

"Could be," Roger said to himself, and added grimly: "Better be."

The telephone bell rang.

"West," said Roger.

"A man's asking for you, sir," said the operator. "He won't speak to anyone else."

"Put him through."

"Is this Inspector West?" a different man asked, gruffly.

"Yes, who is this, please?"

"This is Brown – Bill Brown."

This was it!

Roger said: "Yes, Brown?" and kept his voice level.

"How's my wife?" Brown demanded. "And don't hold out on me."

"I've just come from her," Roger answered. "She's had a bad time, and is seriously ill. She's the worse because she's worried about you, too."

"She always was a worrier," Brown said, gruffly, and then burst out: "I want to see you; how about it?"

"I'm nearly always here," said Roger, "and if I'm not, they know where to find me. Listen to me, Brown. Your wife was nearly killed. When she came round, she was in no state to cover up; she told me everything. Now she's scared out of her wits in case they try to kill you. It –"

"They've already tried," said Bill Brown, flatly.

"All the more reason why –"

"Listen to me for a change," Brown said, roughly. "I'm being watched, see? They've found out where I'm hiding; that's one of the reasons I can't come to see you. If I'm not careful, I'll wind up in the morgue."

He broke off, and there was another sound at the other end of the telephone, followed by a different voice, further away. "Beat *it, Bill. They're comin' !*"

"Brown!" Roger barked.

"Fifty-four Berry Street, Mile End," Brown whispered, urgently. "Come quick, West. If they get me, they'll carve me up."

Roger had the telephone in his hand when the door opened, and a messenger came in.

"Information?" Roger said, quickly. "I want D Division told to surround Berry Street, but to keep out of sight. Have three Flying Squad and two Q cars in the area. Right?"

"Right. Who for?"

"Brown."

"Here's luck!"

"Thanks," Roger said, and stood up. The messenger handed him a sealed envelope marked: URGENT. Roger slit it open, and found a sheet of newsprint with a note from Chatworth, saying, 'Come and see me.' The paper was the *Evening Cry,* half of the front page devoted to news instead of racing.

OUR READERS DEMAND INQUIRY

In response to countless requests from our readers, the Evening Cry is to make representations to the Home Office for a full inquiry into the methods employed by the police following the dismissal of the charges against Mr Paul Raeburn. Our report of the harsh methods used in interrogating Miss Eve Franklin has brought a storm of protest. We publish a selection of letters. Many readers demand the dismissal of Chief Inspector West or at least strong disciplinary action to prevent . . .

Chatworth was alone in his office; big, glowering, with another copy of the front page.

"Well?" he demanded.

Roger said: "I think Brown's cornered in a house in Mile End. I've ordered a concentration, and would like to go there, and take a gun. Have I year permission, sir?"

There was a tense moment of hesitation.

"Come and see me the minute you're back," Chatworth growled.

CHAPTER XVII

54 BERRY STREET

BILL BROWN squeezed out of the telephone kiosk after hanging up on the Yard. The fog was eddying about the crossroads, and he could just see the figure of his friend, Deaken, disappearing along Berry Street. He thought he saw other figures looking out of the darkness, but when he caught up with Deaken, no one else seemed about.

"What did you put the wind up me for?" he demanded.

"I saw a coupla blokes," said Deaken. "Matter o' fact, I *think* I saw four, all near the phone. I'm fed up with this show, that's the truth, Bill. I wish I'd never come with you. Let myself be talked into it, that's what. And – *look out!*"

Two men loomed out of the darkness, and smashed blows at him. He jumped to one side, and ran. Brown swung his left fist at the nearer assailant, and buried it in his stomach. The man backed away, but struck at Brown's head. Brown staggered, kept his balance, fended the man off, and darted in Deaken's wake.

The fog swallowed him up.

He heard thudding footsteps, but could not see more than ten yards in front of him. He struck a lamp-post with his wounded right arm, and winced at the pain, but did not let it slow him down. Number 54 Berry Street was halfway between the kiosk and the main road. His pursuers would not be able to see which house he had entered; if he could once reach 54, he would find sanctuary.

The footsteps stopped.

'Deaken's okay,' thought Brown, slowing down.

He could hear the men coming after him, groping their way through the fog, and then a hollow noise was followed by a vicious oath. One of the men had banged full tilt into the lamp-post.

Brown went into a gateway, trying to see the number on the door of a house. He wasn't quite sure where he was, but couldn't be far away from 54.

"Sixty-two," he muttered.

Now he crept along the pavement, reached Number 54, and found the front door ajar. A man was breathing heavily inside the narrow passage. Deaken's wind had always been short. Brown pushed the door wider open, and stepped inside.

A fist crashed into his face.

The blow came so suddenly, and with such a shock of surprise, that he did not even try to defend himself. He reeled back against the wall, and the man who had struck him appeared from behind the doorway. Deaken was crouching against a door at the foot of the stairs, just out of sight; and he screamed.

The assailant struck Brown across the face. Brown felt blood trickling down his chin, and licked his lips. A third blow banged his head against the wall; another sent a stab of pain up his wounded arm, and he gasped aloud. His assailant grabbed his arm, and began to twist. The pain was so great that Brown felt the strength ebbing from his body.

"Shut that door!" a man ordered.

The front door slammed, and the light went on.

Fog eddied into the hall, but when Brown looked round he could see the men waiting there. They had been hiding in the rooms. The man who had hit him was a hulking fellow, with thick, wet lips, and little porcine eyes. His hands were red and huge. Deaken was in the grip of another man near the stairs. Two others stood by, one of them small and thin-faced; with hair growing far back on his head. The yellow light shone on his forehead and long hooked nose. He was dressed in a suit; the other men were in old Army uniforms.

"Take them upstairs, Andy," said the thin-faced man.

"Okay, Joe," said the big one.

Deaken didn't need 'taking'; he was eager to walk up the stairs. Andy gripped Brown's shoulder, and pushed him forward. Brown felt a warm, sticky patch on his arm where the wound had opened. He was almost too weak with pain to move, but Andy kept kneeing him from behind, and he had to go up.

Andy pushed him into a back room.

"Keep yer trap shut," he ordered.

He stood by the door, towering above both men. Deaken snivelled and began to talk, and Andy clouted him across the face. Deaken dropped on to a camp bed while Brown leaned against the wall, his senses swimming.

It seemed a long time before Joe came into the room, smoothing his bald patch.

Deaken jumped up.

"I don't know nothin'," he screeched. "I don't know a thing. I only come along because –"

"Shut up!" said Joe, and turned to Brown. His little eyes were narrowed and watering, and there was a dewdrop at the end of his nose. He kept rubbing his hands together, making a sliding noise. Andy was breathing noisily through his mouth. The sound of traffic from the Mile End Road was deadened; there was no noise of footsteps outside.

The little house was on a terrace, and the tenant and his family were out. It had been offered to Brown and Deaken while they were on the run, and they had spent the previous night there. The furniture of the bedroom was poor and old-fashioned; the single light was little more than a dim yellow glow; they could have seen almost as well without it, in spite of the fog.

"How did you like what you got, Brown?"Joe inquired, evenly.

Brown said nothing.

"How would you like some *more?*"

"I can give 'im plenty," Andy said.

"That's right – plenty more where that came from," agreed Joe. "Brown, why did you go to Raeburn's flat?"

Brown licked his lips. "I was going to beat him up."

"Why?"

"That's my business."

"We'll see about that," Joe said.

He went for Brown with a rain of blows which made even Deaken cry out in muffled protest. Brown was pushed round the room, trying desperately to defend himself. He kept banging his arm against the wall. His knees felt weak, and now and again he stumbled, but Andy reached forward and hauled him to his feet. By the time Joe stopped, Bill's face was puffy and swollen and streaked with blood; he could hardly get his breath.

"Why did you want to beat Raeburn up?" asked Joe. Brown muttered: "He murdered my brother."

"So you think he murdered your brother. What made you think so, Brown? Don't waste time."

Brown muttered: "Try and find out."

"Bill, he'll bash you again!" cried Deaken.

"Andy," said Joe in a menacing voice, *"you* have a go –"

At the third blow from the giant, Brown began to talk.

He was talking or answering questions for over twenty minutes. Joe learned that Tony had been with Eve on the night of Halliwell's death, and learned exactly what Katie Brown had told Roger. He pressed for more, probing to find out whether Brown could give evidence or whether all he had was hearsay, until Brown was half stupid with pain and fatigue.

"That's fine, that's fine," Joe said, when it was finished. "If you'd told me all that before, you wouldn't have got hurt. Not so much, anyway." He grinned. "But it's a pity you've seen me and my friends, isn't it? Because you'd talk to the narks, wouldn't you? You'd "

A man shouted from downstairs.

Joe swung round. "What's that?"

His answer was a thud and a gasp, and then footsteps sounded on the stairs. Joe moved swiftly toward the door, taking out an automatic. Andy pulled the door open.

A man at the top of the stairs shouted: "Get out of my way, or –"

He broke off, as Joe appeared.

From behind Joe, Andy called: *"West!"*

Joe had kept completely cool during the moments of crisis, and now he said, quite evenly: "You've had it, copper."

He fired.

Roger fired from his pocket as he jumped aside. The other man's bullet smacked into the wall near his head. Joe staggered back, clutching his chest, and his gun dropped from his fingers.

"The cops, *armed,*" breathed Andy. "Gawd!"

CHAPTER XVIII

SILENT JOE

BROWN'S IN hospital but he confirmed his wife's story," said Roger to Chatworth, an hour later. "Deaken's all right, as scared as a rabbit, but not hurt. We've another dish of hearsay evidence, as far as Eve Franklin is concerned, but nothing that leads direct to Raeburn."

"What about this man Joe?" asked Chatworth.

"He's badly hurt. I didn't have time to take aim," said Roger. "He's being operated on now. The other men seem dumb. They say they only know Joe's Christian name, and I haven't been able to find out anything about the man. But I will."

"You'd better. The Home Secretary thinks your resignation would clear the air a lot."

Roger caught his breath. "Are you making me –?"

"I told him if you were suspended, I'd quit," Chatworth said bluffly. "But we want results soon. Yesterday – well, go on."

Roger said, slowly: "Thank you, sir. I think we can get Raeburn eventually, but if you feel that I ought –"

"I said, go on."

Roger said: "Brown says that the man Joe told him he was after Raeburn, but I don't pay much attention to that. We might find a Joe-Tenby connection, and I'm also working on that angle, I don't think we can complain about today's progress."

"No, but this campaign against you must stop soon," Chatworth said.

Roger leaned back in his chair, and drew at his cigarette. He was hungry, his eyes were tired from the strain of driving through the fog, and Chatworth had given him a nasty shock,

"It won't stop until we've dropped the case or got Raeburn," he said. "It's shrewd and very clever – Raeburn flaunting himself as a champion of the rights of the people, and winning a lot of sympathy. But there's a sharp contrast between the newspaper campaign and Raeburn's usual tactics against us, and this violence," Roger went on. "It's almost as if two different people were behind it. Raeburn's completely lost his head, or else he can't control the forces he's let loose. Either way, I think it will give us a break." It had to. "I hope we'll get something out of Joe soon. I've left a man by his side."

Chatworth nodded dismissal.

At half past three, Roger heard that the bullet had been removed, and that Joe was making reasonable progress. He had not yet spoken a word, but if he had a good night he might be questioned the following day.

Tenby was interviewed, but when shown a photograph, professed not to know any Joe. He said that he had been in his rooms all the morning, and certainly he could not be linked up with the attack on Bill Brown on the present evidence. Efforts to identify Joe went on all that day and the following morning, but without result. He seemed to have no history. The other three men, Army deserters, had been staying at a doss house; according to Andy, they had met Joe in a pub.

Joe had paid Andy fifty pounds, and the other two men twenty each for the job.

Roger saw Joe the following afternoon. The wounded man was out of danger, and conscious, but would not say a word. After twenty minutes, Roger gave up, left instructions with the detective on duty in the private ward, and had a talk with the sister in charge.

"There's no reason why he should behave like this," she said, "and he's spoken rationally enough to the nurses, sir. He's had a nasty wound, of course, but –"

"You think he's acting dumb?" asked Roger.

"I do rather think so,"

"Silent Joe," mused Roger. "Well, thanks very much."

He was very thoughtful as he drove away from the hospital.

When Roger reached the Yard, Turnbull and Peel were waiting for him. The two had returned from Brighton in the wake of Raeburn and Eve. Eve had gone to her rooms in Battersea, and Raeburn to the Park Lane flat; both were being kept under observation. They had no idea why Raeburn had changed his plans; he had simply paid his bill after lunch, and driven back. The fog had cleared except in the heart of London, and the journey had been uneventful.

"And you've nothing special to report?" Roger asked.

"There's nothing new at all," admitted Turnbull.

"Well, we've had some luck here," Roger told him, and explained.

"If you ask me, Raeburn's seen the red lights," Turnbull said, with satisfaction.

"That's what I'm hoping."

"But *we* haven't really set them at danger," Turnbull argued. "We haven't done anything to make him rush back to town, anyway."

"No," agreed Roger. "See much of him and Eve?"

"Too much."

"Cooing doves?"

"Coo!" Turnbull grinned. "What's on your mind?"

"You know, apart from Tenby, there's just one known possible witness against Raeburn," Roger said, slowly.

"Yes – our Evie," Turnbull agreed, "but I tell you that pair neck so much they make me heave. Your pal Lessing agrees, too. Eve isn't on any danger list from Raeburn, take it from me."

"I wouldn't be too sure," said Roger. "Well, I'd better get home. How's Lessing?"

"He looks a bit raw," said Turnbull," but he'll survive."

He went off.

Roger tidied up his desk, and was outside by his car when a messenger came hurrying down the steps after him.

"What's on?" Roger asked, and his tension rose.

"A report from Division, sir," the messenger reported. "It says that Mrs Beesley's just gone into Eve Franklin's flat, and the Super thought you ought to know."

CHAPTER XIX

MA BEESLEY TALKS

MA BEESLEY sat on the divan in Eve's bedroom; it was the only thing in the room large enough for her to sit on with comfort. She was dressed in shiny black, which showed up the pasty whiteness of her skin. All the time she talked she smiled, showing her ugly wide-spaced teeth. Now and again, she touched her plaited hair, but not once did she shift her gaze from Eve. Her eyes were wary, half hidden in fat, and her voice was smooth and gentle.

"Now I'm only telling you this for your own good, my dear," she said. "I know Paul Raeburn better than anyone living. You aren't the first, and you won't be the last – you can take that from me. If you're sensible, you'll accept my offer and go away for a few weeks. You'll soon forget him."

Eve did not speak.

"It stands to reason that he's only playing with you, or he wouldn't let you stay in this place," went on Ma, looking about the room. "If he were serious, he'd see that you had a really nice apartment. Haven't you ever thought of that?"

"It's wiser for me to stay here," Eve answered, sullenly.

"Is that what he says?" Ma grinned, knowingly. "He's got an answer for everything, Paul has. I don't want to make a nuisance of myself, my dear, but I'm advising you for your own good. You know the things that have been happening; you know he had to leave

Brighton suddenly. Did he consider you then?"

"He has to attend to business, hasn't he?"

Eve was dressed for out-of-doors, in a two-piece suit of wine red with green braid at the edges and on the sleeves. When Ma Beesley had called, she had been ready to keep an appointment with Paul, but he had sent a message cancelling it; the note had been all that she could have desired. Now this fat harridan was trying to poison her mind. She hated Ma Beesley.

"That's just the point, my dear," wheezed Ma. "Paul has to attend to business, and business always comes first with him. Now you've got a wonderful chance, right here. Five thousand pounds is a lot of money. If you're careful, you can live comfortably on that for a long time. And a pretty girl like you oughtn't to have any difficulty in catching another man. What you want, my dear, is a man who'll marry you."

"That's what *you* think."

Ma leaned forward. "Now don't try to pull the wool over my eyes. You think you can make Paul marry you? Well, you couldn't in a thousand years. If you go away with this money in the bank, you'll be much happier than if you hang on to Paul. I've brought the cash with me." She touched a bulging handbag. "Have a look at it." She opened the bag, peering at Eve as she did so. A thick wad of bank notes rustled in her fingers.

"See those, dear? Take a good look."

"Put the damned money away!" cried Eve. "I'm not going to walk out on Paul, see? You've only come because you know he wants to marry me. What the hell's it got to do with you? I'll show you whether I'm good enough. I'll tell him that you've been here; then you'll see how the land lies."

"Will you?" asked Ma, softly. "I wonder if that would be wise, Eve. I don't want to be unkind, but Paul has a hasty temper, you know –"

"That's what I mean!"

"He won't vent it on me," said Ma, confidently. "You see, he relies on me for everything, duck – for everything. He knows that anything I do is always in his interest. I can handle Paul, but you can't. I don't ask you to decide too quickly, but think about it."

"I don't need to think about it!"

"I see," said Ma. She stood up, putting the money back in her bag. "You're very silly, Eve. I've told you what's good for you, and I'm right. The further you keep from Paul in the next few weeks, the better for you. He's very worried, and he isn't interested in anything but business, and in keeping quite clear of the police. People who might do him harm get hurt, my dear. Don't forget your Tony. He was murdered –"

Eve cried: "That's a lie!"

"Well, he died in very mysterious circumstances," murmured Ma. "Don't you think –?"

The ringing of the front-door bell cut across her words, and they stared toward the little hall. Eve's hands were tightly clenched, and the fat woman was frowning.

"Who do you think that is?"

"I don't know," muttered Eve. "I don't want to see anyone. You – you've been lying to me, you needn't deny it. You just want to separate us; you don't care how you do it. Paul wouldn't –"

Ma raised a hand, and snapped her fingers beneath the girl's nose. "Anyone out there can hear what we say, you fool," Ma whispered. "Open the door, quick, and don't let them know I'm here." When Eve hesitated she pushed her toward the door. "Don't keep them waiting."

The bell rang again. Eve went into the hall, feeling weak and listless; the old beast had shocked her so. She could only think of one word: *murder*. She had always been sure that Tony had committed suicide, had never believed in the accident theory, but murder!

She opened the door.

"Good evening, Miss Franklin," said Roger West.

It was obvious to Roger that something had happened to upset Eve Franklin badly. Her hands were unsteady, and her eyes were feverishly bright. It was not the shock of seeing him; in fact, she peered at him for a moment without recognition. Then she drew back.

Roger saw a big shadow against the door of the inner room; Ma Beesley probably did not want it known that she was here. He smiled as he stepped into the hall.

"I'm afraid I have to worry you again," he said. "Come in, Peel."

The girl backed toward the inner door, the colour draining from her face as the two men entered. "What – what do you want?"

"I just want the truth out of you," Roger said.

Then Eve was glad to see Ma Beesley, for the fat woman appeared in the doorway, all creases and double chins.

"I think we all realise that you would like to *frighten* the poor child," she bleated. "Don't take on, Eve, don't let them bully you."

She squeezed through the doorway and came to Eve's side, smiling her set smile, but her little eyes were hostile. She touched Eve's arm, and the girl shrank away. There was no time to lose, if Roger was to get any advantage; he sensed that there had been a quarrel; that the older woman had frightened the girl; working on that might give him the best chance of breaking Eve down.

"That's enough from you," he said. "I want to see Miss Franklin alone."

"I daresay you do, but you can't," retorted Ma. "I know better than that. I'm not frightened of a policeman. I came here to try to help the poor child –"

"Help!" gasped Eve.

"We don't see eye to eye, my dear, but I came with the best intentions," said Ma Beesley. "You really ought to come in and sit down." She looked at Roger insolently. "You're not going to insist on seeing her alone, are you? Because if you are, I shall have to telephone her solicitor immediately. Mr. Warrender had to do that once before, remember?"

"You'll find you're making a mistake," Roger said, roughly.

"I think you nearly made one," retorted Ma Beesley. "Now, if you really want to help the poor child, come and listen to me." She led the way into the sitting-room.

Roger glanced at Peel. "Stay here," he said. Peel nodded, and then gave a gesture of resignation.

Ma led the girl to the divan, and pushed her gently down on to it, then lowered herself to a chair beside her; she overlapped the chair which creaked noisily.

"I've been trying to advise Eve for her own good," she told Roger. "She'll tell you the same, too, although she doesn't agree with what I say, I want her to break with Paul Raeburn, Mr West."

"To *break* with him?"

"That's right. I can talk to you, anyhow," she went on, leaning forward. "You're a man of the world, and I needn't be afraid of shocking you! I know Paul. He's a nice fellow in a lot of ways, but he isn't a one-woman man, if you know what I mean. I've told Eve it will save her a lot of heartache later on if she takes the plunge and leaves him now, instead of waiting for him to tire of her. He's very busy, and he won't have much time for her in the next week or two." There was a barb in those words, although she uttered them so smoothly. "And it's now or never, I think."

Roger didn't speak; she had completely surprised him.

"After all, I *am* a woman," continued Ma Beesley. "My time for romance may be past" – she gave a broad grin – "but I know just what Eve feels like, and I want to save her from being hurt. Now be honest, Chief Inspector. Do you think that she will come to any good if she continues to associate with him?"

"Would he like to hear you say that?" asked Roger, sourly. She was as cunning as a witch.

Ma sniggered. "He wouldn't be at all surprised. I never mince my words with Paul. He might be annoyed, but he'd soon get over it, and there are plenty of other fish in the sea. Now don't be unkind, Chief Inspector; give me your honest opinion."

Roger said: "You want to talk to the Welfare Officer, not to me, Ma."

"Oh dear," Ma sighed. "So few men have the courage of their convictions. I know in your heart you agree with me, and you think it would be wise for Eve to make a break *now*. I can't do more than I've done," she added virtuously, "and I only hope that she'll listen to me. Eve dear, do you think you could let me have a shakedown for the night? I don't like to leave you here alone in your present frame of mind."

She was saying that she meant to prevent Roger from interviewing the girl alone.

"Oh, I don't care what you do," muttered Eve, weakly.

"Then I will stay, dear," said Ma Beesley, and beamed at Roger. "You can tell that handsome young man outside that he can have a good night's sleep; he needn't worry about following me any more tonight!"

"I haven't quite finished," said Roger.

"Oh, I'm sorry. What is it you have to say?"

Roger said: "You'll hear in due course." He turned to Eve, pulled up a chair, and sat down. He did all this very slowly, looking only at the girl, "Miss Franklin, I want to help you in every way I can. You have got yourself into an extremely difficult situation, and if I were you I wouldn't rely too much on your new friends."

"But I've just been telling her how delicate her situation is," protested Ma Beesley. "You might as well have agreed with me in the first place."

Roger sat looking at her, and gradually began to smile. That puzzled Ma, until at last she looked away. Eve was staring at her reflection in the mirror.

"Happy, Ma, aren't you?" asked Roger.

Ma didn't answer.

"And you really came here to advise Eve to leave Raeburn," marvelled Roger. "How much did you offer as a bribe?"

"Now, Chief Inspector –"

"And why are you so anxious to separate them?"

"I've told you," said Ma Beesley, sharply. "I don't intend to say any more about it."

"But you tried to buy Eve off," murmured Roger. "Very interesting. How much?"

"I want to help –" Ma began.

"You've never willingly helped anyone in your life," Said Roger. "Miss Franklin, you're in a much worse position than you realise. We are watching you for your own good, and don't hesitate to call on me if this woman or any of her friends frightens you."

He had jolted them both, and this was the moment to leave. He glared at Ma, and turned on his heel.

Peel spoke as they went downstairs. "She's a nasty piece of work, that Ma Beesley." Roger nodded. "Do you want me to stay and watch her?"

"Yes, and I want the flat watched, too. I don't think Ma will stay all night," said Roger. "There isn't a telephone at the apartment, but I wouldn't be surprised if Ma doesn't get hold of someone else to take over. None of them will want Eve to be interviewed tonight."

"You shook the girl all right," said Peel. "I heard everything and saw a lot."

"She'd already had a shaking," Roger reflected. "What time are you due for relief?"

"Midnight, sir."

"All right – good luck."

When Roger's car had disappeared, Peel strolled up and down the street, glancing at the lighted window of Eve's apartment. He was thinking more about Roger West than of either of the women, for Handsome had something which Peel could not define. He remembered the bleakness on Roger's face, followed by the sudden change, and the smile which suggested a confidence that he could not possibly have felt. But it had worried the fat slug, and they'd come out even, after all.

Peel kept walking up and down; the cold soon made him think of hot grog and a blazing fire. As the time wore on, he doubted whether either woman would leave the house that night.

Peel was wrong. Ma Beesley left the apartment a little after ten o'clock. She did not look up and down the street, although she must have known that she was being followed. She waddled toward the corner where there was a dimly lit telephone kiosk, pulled open the heavy door, and squeezed into the box.

She could not close the door on her bulk. That did not seem to trouble her. She had some coppers in her hand, and twisted her body, so that she could insert them and use the dial. Keeping in the shadows, Peel went as near as he dared. He could actually hear the whir of the dial after the pennies had dropped. He saw Ma peering through the window away from him; she seemed determined to ignore him.

"Hallo, George," she said, clearly.

"Warrender," Peel muttered.

"Yes, George, it's me," went on Ma Beesley. "I couldn't phone before, because I've had a little trouble with Eve. That dreadful West man came and questioned her again, and I had to see that she was all right. I think someone ought to spend the night here."

There was a pause.

"Well, I will if there's no one else," said Ma. "Yes . . . yes, I would like a word with Paul. . . . Hallo, Paul!" Ma's voice oozed syrup. "Yes, I spoke to her about it . . . she wouldn't accept the offer . . . you see, she's very loyal. . . . Oh, yes, I tried, but she wouldn't agree; she doesn't believe that you're so fickle!" Ala sniggered. "Yes, Paul, I'll stay."

She rang off, edged herself out of the box, and approached Peel, who was hiding in the shadows of a house. She plodded along the pavement, and he could hear her wheezing. She drew level with him, and passed. "She hasn't seen me," thought Peel.

She turned and looked over her shoulder.

"Isn't it a dark night?" she remarked, and padded on. Peel swore at her under his breath, and waited until she had gone into the house before he telephoned the Yard, and asked for a message to be sent to Handsome West.

Peel himself couldn't make head or tail of the situation. Why had Ma Beesley come to pay the girl off, and then reported her failure to Raeburn?

Katie Brown was subdued when Roger went to see her again at the Putney hospital, next day. She said she was relieved that Bill was 'inside', and hoped he would stay there until the affair was over, but obviously she hated all thought of it. Yes, of course, she wanted to help as much as she could, she said, and the doctor had declared her fit enough to leave hospital.

Roger gave her a cigarette, as he asked: "Do you still remember the voice of the man on the Common?"

"Shall I ever forget it!"

"I want you to listen to a man speaking, and to tell me whether you recognise the voice," Roger said. "Will you do that?"

"Of course I will."

"He met with an accident, and may look a mess," Roger told her, "but don't worry."

As they neared Joe's ward at the City Hospital, the matron caught sight of Roger, and hurried across. She was a great talker, and reported earnestly that she was worried because Joe was making no progress. She thought that he was pretending to be more ill than he really was, and although he still said little and showed no interest in anything, he ate well enough: that was the only satisfactory thing to report. And – this was the main burden of her story – did Mr. West think that the policeman could be removed from the ward for a few hours? It might be possible to judge the patient's real condition, then.

"I'll see what I can do," promised Roger. "Does he still talk to the nurses?"

"A word or two, that's all."

"I wonder if you'll go and have a word with him now," Roger said. "I'd like you to leave the door open, so that I can hear."

The matron nodded, went in, and spoke cheerfully to the invalid. At first, Joe answered only in monosyllables which could hardly be heard. Gradually, his voice strengthened, until he said clearly: "I tell you I don't want anything else, get the hell out of here!"

Katie gasped: *"That's him! That's his voice!"*

"Quiet," whispered Roger.

Katie gripped his arm tightly, and stood staring at the door.

It was a help, another piece in the puzzle, but it did not lead to Raeburn.

Roger made time to go through all the evidence in any way connected with Raeburn, and to summarise and analyse it. There was still little to enthuse over. The Yard's foremost solicitor agreed that it would be folly to put Bill Brown into the witness box against

Eve; although there were no convictions against Brown, he had committed dozens of petty offences, and Abel Melville would find little difficulty in discrediting him in court. Even a confession of guilt from Eve would have its drawbacks; and, as the solicitor pointed out, they had to prove not only that Eve had lied, but that Raeburn had been a party to her perjury. That was going to be the difficulty.

Joe remained a man without an identity. The East End Divisions were working at pressure to try to discover more about him, but there was no evidence that he lived in this district. Andy and the other men who had been caught at Berry Street were still on remand.

Tenby continued to spend most of his leisure in The Lion at Chelsea; Mark Lessing, his face better, went there several times, but Tenby was always on his own.

Raeburn and Warrender spent a great deal of time at the City offices of Raeburn Investments, ostensibly occupied with legitimate business. Ma Beesley stirred from Park Lane only to do the shopping. Eve remained at her apartment for two days on end, and Roger began to hope that Raeburn had thrown her over. If he had, out of sheer vindictiveness, she might tell all she knew.

On the third evening she left her apartment, entered the Silver Wraith, and went to the Silver Kettle. All seemed well again between her and Raeburn; they danced cheek to cheek much of the time.

The newspapers either dropped the story of Katie and the Browns, or kept it alive with small paragraphs. The next opportunity to use the Press would be when Bill Brown came up for the second hearing, in two days' time.

"I'd like to know more than we do now, before we have another publicity splash," Roger said to Turnbull. "I think we'll ask for a second eight days in custody."

"Brown won't object, that's certain," Turnbull said.

"We've found the connection between Brown and Raeburn; we can prove that Joe attacked Brown, so what we need most is a connecting link between Raeburn and Joe," Roger went on.

"Very original," Turnbull jeered, and smacked a fist into a thick palm, exasperatedly. "I never seem to be able to get my teeth into the job; it's like nibbling at an apple on a string with your hands tied behind your back." He paused, and then his voice grew louder. "Here, Handsome, we've been slow as tortoises!" His eyes positively blazed.

"Which way this time?"

"We ought to take *Tenby* along to see Joe," breathed Turnbull. "It would tear them apart if they know each other."

"Good idea, and I'll fix it tomorrow," Roger said, and grinned. "Tonight I've promised to take Janet to the pictures."

"If anyone needs a night off, you do," Turnbull agreed, unexpectedly.

Roger was feeling more cheerful and relaxed, when he walked home with Janet from the cinema. They went the long way round by the river and, in spite of a chilling east wind, stood watching the lights of the bridges and the south bank reflected on the water. A fleet of barges moved slowly up-Thames, and the waves from their wake splashed lazily against the embankment.

"I'm told that Raeburn's just bought a coastal shipping line," Roger remarked.

"Oh, forget Raeburn!" Janet exploded.

Roger chuckled. "Perhaps he'll drown himself," he said, tightening his grip about her waist. "It's getting cold, sweet, let's get going!"

They turned the corner, and saw light streaming from a doorway halfway along Bell Street. Someone was standing at a gate, peering in the other direction, and as they drew nearer Janet said sharply; "Roger, that's Scoopy!"

She broke into a run, calling, "Scoop! Is Richard all right?"

"Course he is," said Scoopy, scornfully. "It's an urgent message for Dad, that's all. A man rang up three times for you, Dad, and the last time gave me the message: 'Look after Eve', he said, and said you'd know what he meant."

CHAPTER XX

'LOOK AFTER EVE'

THERE WAS the message, written on the corner of a newspaper in Scoopy's clear hand. The first call had come at a quarter to nine, the second at half past, and the third at five minutes to ten, when the man had left the message.

"You're sure it was a man?" asked Roger, urgently.

"Well, it sounded like one," Scoopy said. "I suppose it could have been a woman with a deep voice, now I come to think of it. I didn't know what to do. Old Fish was tired; he's asleep, I think."

"You did fine," Roger said. I'd better check on Evie. Make me some tea, pet, will you, and a few sandwiches."

Janet started to say; "Must you?" but checked herself.

Turnbull was still at the Yard when Roger telephoned. "Who's watching Eve tonight?" asked Roger.

"Allen and McKinley," Turnbull answered. "Allen's at the front – McKinley's the younger, if there's any climbing over garden walls, he's the one for it. Shall I double the watch?"

"Yes, and we'll go there ourselves," said Roger.

"This may be a hoax," Turnbull pointed out.

"I don't think that anyone in this business is likely to play that kind of hoax," said Roger. "Have you got a report on where Eve has been tonight?"

"Just a minute –" said Turnbull.

He was away from the telephone for some time. Janet came in, and stood in front of the mirror, poking her fingers through her hair.

"Hallo, Handsome," said Turnbull at last. "She's been with Raeburn to the Silver Kettle, but left early. She reached her apartment at eleven-fifteen – that report was sent in twenty minutes ago. Nothing else."

"Get all reports checked," said Roger. "I'll come right away."

He reached the Yard at midnight, and found that Turnbull had made a full summary of the night's reports. He studied them closely. Ma Beesley had not left Park Lane, and Warrender had not arrived at the flat until after ten o'clock. Tenby

"This might be interesting." Turnbull tapped the report.

Tenby had been at The Lion until half past eighty when he had left and boarded a Number 11 bus at Sloane Square. The detective watching him had not been able to board the bus, so had reported and gone back to The Lion; Tenby had not returned. His boarding house was being watched, but there was no news from the man who was stationed at Fulham Road.

"The Number 11 passes Raeburn Investments office," Turnbull remembered, "and Warrender may have been there, as he arrived home late."

"Let's check the report on Warrender again," said Roger. "H'm – it's not Peel's; it's from the man on duty at Park Lane. Peel was watching Warrender tonight, wasn't he?"

"Yes."

"And no report."

"He hasn't had much time," Turnbull said. "He may have gone home; there wouldn't be any need to hurry about a routine report. Shall I ring him?"

Roger nodded.

Turnbull put in the call, and then replaced the receiver. They went over the reports again, very carefully, and Roger answered when the telephone bell rang.

A woman with a frail voice spoke from the other end, "Hallo?"

"Is Detective Officer Peel there, please?"

"No, sir, he isn't," answered the woman. "I'm getting just a little worried; he said he would be in by half past ten tonight, or else let me know. He hasn't rung up."

"I'm afraid he's been kept working late," Roger said, reassuringly. "Who is this speaking?"

"Why, his mother, Mrs Peel."

"Thank you very much, Mrs Peel. If he does come in during the next quarter of an hour, ask him to ring the Yard and ask for Chief Inspector West, will you? . . . Thanks, very much." He put the receiver down, frowning, and remarked: "I don't like that."

"He might have dodged off on some line of his own," said Turnbull.

"Wouldn't be like Peel," declared Roger. "I think I'll go to see Eve. You take a man with you, and have a look round the outside of Raeburn's offices. You'd better have a word with the City Police first."

"Mustn't tread on their corns, eh? Okay," Turnbull said.

The City of London was quiet as Turnbull drove through it with a detective officer by his side. They passed three policemen at different points, but the streets were practically deserted. The tall buildings were in darkness, and the narrow alleys leading off the main streets were invisible.

Turnbull saw two men standing at a corner, and pulled up. One was in uniform, and the other in plain clothes; they were two City policemen who had arranged to meet him on this corner. Raeburn Estates offices were in a modern building which had been damaged during the last war; one part was still uninhabitable, with gaping windows and crumbling walls.

"Hallo, Mr Turnbull."

"Hallo, Wray." Turnbull was hearty. "Anything for me?"

"I've had no report of any trouble about here, although we've been keeping a close watch," Wray answered. "Your man, Peel, was here until half past nine."

"Sure?"

If Tenby had come here, he would have arrived about nine-fifteen.

"He was last seen when the rounds were made at nine," said Wray. "That means he was here between nine-ten and nine-twenty."

"Where did he stand?"

"In the bombed-out front," said Wray, leading the way along the street. "He had a word with my man, and said he was going to finish some tea he had in a flask; it was pretty nippy." They reached the gaping window of the damaged office; beyond it, piles of rubble were just visible in the light of a street lamp. "He wasn't here when my man went round next time," continued Wray, "but he was due off duty at ten o'clock, wasn't he?"

"Not tonight," said Turnbull. "A chap he wanted was here, and Peel is the type to stay all night." Wray gave him a hand, and he climbed on to a window sill. "Lend me a torch, will you?"

Wray climbed through and shone a torch about the scorched walls and the untidy rubble. They scrambled over the debris toward the far corner, where two walls formed a narrow passage.

"This is as far as it goes," Wray said, as he reached the passage. "If he's not –"

The light of the torch shone upon the inert figure of a man. It was Peel.

At first Turnbull thought that the young DO was dead, He had been knocked over the head savagely, and did not seem to be breathing. A policeman went for an ambulance, as Turnbull and Wray examined the victim in the torchlight. He was breathing after all, and raising his eyelids, Turnbull saw that the pupils were pinpoints.

"Looks like a drug," he growled. "Knocked out first, and then given the needle."

"Drugs are new in this case, aren't they?" Wray asked.

"They've been used once before," Turnbull remembered. "And on Peel."

For Peel had been ill after drinking with Tenby.

A light shone under the door of Eve's apartment, or even Roger would have hesitated about knocking so late at flight. She opened the door, and stood staring in the semidarkness, for she had not switched on the hall light. He noticed that she clutched the door.

"Who – who is it?"

"West," Roger said, brusquely.

There was a pause. Then: "Why, Handsome!" The giggle which followed surprised Roger as much as the 'Handsome'.

"What a time of night to come and see a lady! Come – come in!" She flung the door wide open, and backed away, unsteadily, "I *hate* drinking alone," she went on. "Come – come an' have one. Yush – Yush a li'l one!" She put a hand on his shoulder, and pushed him toward the sitting-room. "Don't be shy – I'm quite nishe, really!"

Her hair was neat on one side, and falling loose on the other; she had lacked off her shoes and, judging from the gin bottle and the glass on the table, had been lying on the settee, drinking herself stupid. Her cheeks were flushed, almost as red as her scarlet dressing gown, and her eyes glowed wickedly.

"What'll you have?" she asked, and giggled again. "I've only got gin. Have a gin?"

"Not now, thanks."

"Oh, don't be a stiffneck. A little drop o' gin' never hurt a man yet. Look at me – I've had a lot of li'l drops!" She went to a cupboard, and took out another glass. "Drowning my sorrows, that's what I'm doing," she said. "Nice way to drown, isn't it? *Do* have a drink." She picked up the bottle, but gin spilled out on the floor. "S'no use," she said, and waved airily. "Help yourself."

She flopped on to the divan.

Roger poured a little gin into a glass, put the bottle down, and glanced over his shoulder. DO Allen was on the landing; he hoped the man would have the sense to come into the hall, so that he could hear what went on.

"Don't be *mean*" protested Eve. "Pour me out a li'l one, too."

Roger obliged.

"Now let's be friendly," said Eve, coyly. "Come 'n sit down. You know-" she looked at him with her eyes brimming over with mirth – "you know I don't like being bad friends with a good-looking man.

It's not like *me*. Did anyone ever tell you how handsome you are, Handsome?" She giggled. "Paul told me that they call you Handsome."

"Just his joke." Roger did not sit down, and she seemed to forget her invitation.

"It's the truth," she assured him, earnestly. "Nice eyes, nice nose, nice mouth, pretty hair – I'll bet you've got a fat wife! Like Ma – ugh! Do you know, I positively hate Ma. Old bitchy-witchy Ma. Hate her. Always did,' and always will."

"A lot of people don't like her," said Roger.

"Fat old sow," declared Eve. "I think Paul's going to fire her."

"Is he?" My God;

"He as good as said he was fed up to the back teeth with her," Eve told him. "Handsome, dear – come right here." She put out a hand, took his, and pulled him toward her. "Secret," she whispered gravely, close to his ear. "Promise you won't tell."

"Cross my heart."

"Paul an' me are *engaged*!" She kissed his ear. "Isn't that wonderful? Wonderful! I can hardly believe it I thought he was cooling off. Bitchy-witchy Ma scared me. Said he would get tired of me. Fat lot she knew!" She put her hands against his cheeks and squeezed his face. "Isn't it wunnerful?"

"Wonderful."

"I knew you would understand," Eve said, solemnly. "I knew you weren't the sourpuss you pretended to be. Me and Paul!" She pressed her nose against his. "I'll have everything I want – every blooming thing! He had to leave me early tonight; he's sush a busy man, so I had to come home alone. Couldn't sit here and do *nothing*; couldn't go out, so – I had a li'l drink, and another li'l drink won't do you any harm!" She began to croon, swaying from side to side. "I've never been so happy, all my dreams come true!"

Roger freed himself. "So there's nothing more you want?" he asked, lightly.

"That's exactly right – except to get rid of bitchywitchy Ma. And I will, before I've finished. You know what? She knows she won't las' a month after I get establish' as the lady of the house, so she tried to buy me off. Offered me five thousand quid – I *saw* it. In beautiful notes, too. Why, that was the lash time you were here. You didn't know you were standing next to a cool five thousand, did you, Handsome?"

"I certainly didn't. Did Ma want anything else?"

"I wouldn't like to say what she really wanted; you can never tell with a creashure like that."

"When's the great day to be?" Roger asked.

"Soon," crowed Eve. "He promised me that it wouldn't be long. He's handling some very big bishiness deals just now, and as soon as they're finished, we're going to elope! He's given me the address of a li'l country cottage where we'll meet, and then – whoops!"

"I've often wanted to live in the country," Roger remarked, casually. "Whereabouts are you going?"

"Thash *another* secret," Eve declared, and laughed in his face. " I'm not as drunk as I seem, Handsome, you needn't think you can get anything out of me. Boyo! What a night! Do you know wha'? I'm going dizzy! The room's going round and round and your eyesh are getting closer together; you look jush like a monkey. Ha-ha-ha! Handsome Wesh looks like a monkey – whoops!"

She fell back on the pillows, looking at him through her lashes, and seemed to be laughing at him. Her lips were pursed provocatively; she held her head a little to one side. "Handsome," she cooed.

"Yes?"

"You haven't even tol' me why you came to see me."

"I just wanted to make sure you were safe. I've been worried about you ever since Tony's murder."

"*Murder?*" she echoed, in a squeaky voice; the word seemed to have sobered her in a flash. "Did you say *murder?*"

Roger said: "Well-"

"That's what *she* said," said Eve, deliberately, "but I don't really believe it. Paul wouldn't allow a wicked thing like that. Tony killed himself because I had turned him down, that's what happened." She straightened up. "Handsome, tell me he wasn't murdered."

Roger said carefully: "Officially, it was accidental death. I think he was murdered because he knew too .much, and I think that anyone who knows the same thing is in danger. Tony's brother knew, and he was attacked. Kate-you know Katie Brown-"

"Puddeny little piece," muttered Eve, no longer on top of the world.

"You heard what happened to her, simply because of what she knew," said Roger. "That's why I come to see you so often. We want to look after you. You're mixed up with a queer lot of people, Eve."

"That's not Paul's fault! Paul's all right, he's wonderful! It's that old woman and Warrender. I don't trust either of them. Do you hear me, if anything happened it was their fault – not Paul's. I – but I don't believe it," she added, abruptly. "I think you're trying to scare me." She glared. "I don't want you bloody police coming and worrying me at all hours of the night, it's not right. If I told Paul, he'd make you sit up!"

"Eve," said Roger, in a voice which startled her. "I came to warn you that you might be in danger. Don't take anything for granted. Don't try to evade the men who are watching you – they're looking after you, not trying to trap you. Don't forget it."

She was shocked into silence.

"Good night," said Roger.

He turned and went out of the room. Allen, a stocky, plump man of forty, was standing in the hall, and obviously had heard every word of the conversation. He opened the front door for Roger, and then went downstairs. Allen made no comment until they reached the street. Then a car drew up, and Turnbull put his head out of the window. "We've found Peel," he announced.

Roger forced his thoughts from Eve Franklin, and listened to Turnbull's story.

A doctor at the City Hospital had seen Peel, and believed that he had been given a powerful narcotic; it was too early to say whether he was in a dangerous condition.

"As far as I can make out from the City chaps, Peel went into a damaged office to take a drink from his thermos flask," explained Turnbull. "He probably found it a useful hiding place. It looks as if he had been watched, and someone was waiting in that passage and hit him when his back was turned."

"And it also looks as if Tenby went to see Warrender, and didn't want to be seen," said Roger. "Past time we saw Tenby again."

"Tonight?"

"Right now."

"That's better," Turnbull said. "Let's go."

CHAPTER XXI

TENBY IS INDIGNANT

T ENBY BLINKED at Roger and Turnbull in the bright light of his bedroom. His landlady, a small, tight lipped woman, stood on the landing. She had protested against being awakened at half past twelve, complained bitterly about her lodger being disturbed, and argued all the time they walked up the long narrow flight of stairs to the third floor where Tenby had his room. The house was clean, but needed repainting and repapering. Tenby's room was large and tidy. There was an old-fashioned iron bedstead with brass knobs at the corners, a huge Victorian dressing table, and a large wardrobe. On a bamboo bedside table was a broken slab of chocolate. Tenby himself was in faded blue-striped pyjamas which were too small for him, and showed that he had a potbelly.

He rubbed his eyes. "Yes, yes, I know," he said. "Yes, o' course. It's all right, Mrs Reed, don't worry." He yawned, and stood back. "Come in, gentlemen. I'm sorry I'm not properly awake yet. 'Ave a seat."

"We'll stand," said Roger.

"All right, please yourself," retorted Tenby. "I'm going to sit down." He dropped into an old-fashioned armchair. "Now, what's it all about? I didn't want to kick up a stink wiv the old dragon about, but it's a bit 'ot, coming here at this time o' night."

"Where have you been tonight?" Roger demanded.

" Minding me own – the same as you oughter."

"You were at The Lion, in Chelsea, until half past eight. Where did you go after that?"

"Oh, so you've been spying on me, 'ave yer?" Tenby was truculent. "I'm going to lodge a complaint, that's what I'm going to do. Where I go is me own business, and you needn't think I'm going to tell *you.*"

Roger looked at Turnbull. "We'd better take him along."

"And break his neck on the way."

"You can flicking well think again," snapped Tenby. "I'm staying here."

"You're coming to the Yard to make a statement about your movements tonight," said Roger. "Put some clothes on."

"I tell you-"

"If you won't put some clothes on, we'll wrap you up in a blanket and carry you downstairs. Don't argue. You'll tell us where you've been tonight, or you'll come along with us to the Yard."

Tenby looked at him, insolently. "Okay, I'll come," he said, "but you 'aven't 'eard the last o' this, Mr Ruddy West."

He got up and began to dress.

Obviously, he was worried, and his truculence sprang from the effort to hide his anxiety. He dressed slowly and deliberately. Now and again, his gaze wandered to a corner cabinet, but it did not linger for long; obviously, he had not expected tonight's visit. A search of the room might yield a stock of drugs, as Tenby had once been a chemist, but without a search warrant it wasn't worth the risk. A man could stay outside, and make sure that no one else entered the room.

"Well, *I'm* ready," said Tenby, at last.

In his car Roger kept glancing at his passenger, but Tenby stared haughtily ahead. This was the man who might be much cleverer than the police realised; he might have murdered Tony Brown, and been responsible for the attack on Bill Brown – *if* the police theory was right.

At the Yard, Turnbull went to Information, and Roger took Tenby along to his office, and then sent for a shorthand writer.

Tenby's continued silence began to irritate him; he was suspicious of a trick, and watched his words carefully.

"Now, let's have it. Where have you been tonight?"

"What's the charge?" demanded Tenby.

"If I make a charge, you'll soon find out."

"I don't want any more of your lip," sneered Tenby. "I'm not going to make no statement, but I'm going to raise hell about being dragged out of bed at this time o' night."

Roger said: "So you formally refuse to tell us where you've been tonight?"

"And what are you going to do about it ?" sneered Tenby.

"Make a note of that," Roger said to a sergeant. He leaned back in his chair, and looked at the man standing in front of him. "I want to know something else," he went on. "Do you remember the night of October 31?"

"Why should I remember any particular night?" demanded Tenby. "You ruddy dicks are all the same, just because I had a bit of luck-"

"I'm not so sure that Odds-on Pools are as lucky for you as you think," interrupted Roger. "October 31 was a Wednesday, the night that Tony Brown was gassed in his room at Battersea. Remember Brown?"

"Yes, and I knew a man named Smith once."

"The day will come when you won't feel so smart," said Roger. "Let me remind you about the 31st of October again. You weren't at The Lion all that evening. You weren't at home. Your landlady has been questioned, and she knows you were out. None of your friends know where you were, but you were reported to be in Battersea Park."

"That's a lie!" Tenby's voice rose.

"We'll find out whether it's true or not. If you weren't in the park, where were you?"

"You don't expect me to remember where I am *every* night, do you?"

"I think you remember that particular night," said Roger. "You refuse to tell me that, too – that right?"

"I tell you I don't remember!"

Roger glanced at the shorthand writer.

"Got that, Sergeant?"

"Yes, sir."

"All right, Tenby, I shan't hold you – yet. But you're in big trouble, unless you remember where you were on the night of the 31st of October."

Tenby's little eyes were looking everywhere but at Roger, and his hands were working. The sergeant stood stolidly by.

"Get going," Roger said, roughly.

Tenby hesitated.

"Well?" asked Roger, abruptly.

"I can't remember what happened nearly three weeks ago," Tenby muttered. "Tonight-"

"Yes?"

"I was out seeing some of me old friends. Just because I've 'ad a bit o' luck, it doesn't mean that I drop me old friends like 'ot cakes. Wouldn't be fair." Tenby became virtuous. "I got a Number 11 to the Bank, and then picked up a 13 to Algit. That's where I was, see? If you'd asked me decently, I would have told you right from the beginning."

"Where did you go?" demanded Roger.

"The Three Bells."

"What time did you arrive there?"

"Round about ten, I s'pose."

"It doesn't take an hour and a half to get from Chelsea to Aldgate."

"I 'ad to wait for a bus-"

"There's a good bus service," said Roger, coldly, leaning back in his chair. "Have you seen Warrender tonight, Tenby?"

"Who?"

"George Warrender. Raeburn's secretary."

"Now, listen," said Tenby, earnestly. "I wouldn't go to see that geezer if you was to offer me a five-pound note. I did a few jobs for them once, mind you. When Raeburn bought 'is dog-racing tracks, I kept an eye open for them before the races, to see there wasn't no funny business with the dogs. But d'you know what? They wanted me to dope the dogs. *Me!* I soon sheered off *them*. Mind you, they didn't come out in the open; a lot of 'ints, that's all there was, but it told me plenty. I don't interfere with a man's sport, Mr West, you can take that from me. Why, I 'aven't done a stroke of work for Warrender or Raeburn since then – you can ask them if you like. They can't say no different."

"And you haven't seen Warrender tonight?"

"Of course I haven't!" Tenby rubbed his hands together, nervously. "Listen, Mr West, I'll tell you what *did* happen tonight, Gawd's truth. I 'ad a telephone message at The Lion, a man asked me to meet him at Algit Pump, see? 'E said he was a friend of a friend. 'E said he'd got a dead cert for me at Birmingham, so I said I'd go along. I was early and he was late, that's how it was I was so long getting to The Three Bells. This bloke wanted me to lend 'im some money – that was the truth of it. You'd be surprised the tricks they get up to. I'm sorry I can't account for where I was every minute of the evening, but that's the truth, Mr West."

"It had better be," Roger said, grimly.

"And if you'd been as friendly when you woke me up as you are now-"

"You'd have lied to me then, instead of now," said Roger. "You won't get away with murder, Tenby."

"Why, I never said a word about – about murder!" Tenby jumped up. "It's not fair, Mr West, picking on me like this just because I 'ad a bit o' luck!"

"Tony Brown didn't have much luck."

"I never knew there was such a man until I read about him in the paper," protested Tenby. "I've told you the solemn truth, Mr West. I give you my oath on it."

"All right. I'll want you back here to sign a statement in the morning," Roger said. "You can make up your mind about any additions by then."

"I don't mind what I sign," declared Tenby. "I want to make things as easy as I can. But you take my advice, Mr West, and don't trust that Warrender or that Raeburn. They're nasty pieces o' work."

"I know a lot of nasty pieces of work," said Roger, and Tenby gave up.

Roger sent a sergeant to drive him back.

There was the gap which Tenby could not account for, and a lot could happen in three-quarters of an hour. Roger made a note to inquire from the landlord of The Lion whether there had been a telephone message, and, after a few minutes' talk with Turnbull, went home.

Peel's condition was unchanged.

Before Tenby arrived next morning, the landlord of The Lion confirmed that the man had been called to the telephone; that part of his story seemed true. But why had he refused to tell it earlier? In the cold light of morning, Roger found another important question: why had Tenby's manner changed so abruptly? Had he been knocked completely off balance by the talk of Tony Brown's murder?

Undoubtedly, Tenby had been at The Three Bells, Aldgate, at ten o'clock, but his movements between those critical hours of nine and ten could not be checked. There were no grounds for making a charge, or even searching his rooms. If anything had been concealed in the corner, it would almost certainly be gone by now.

Nothing else had happened at Eve's apartment.

Raeburn and Warrender reached the City office together soon after ten o'clock; that was normal enough.

Roger had a telephoned report about that at a quarter to eleven, and was then told that Tenby was waiting to see him. The statement was already typed out. Roger went along to a waiting-room, and the little man signed before witnesses. His manner was calmer, and more ingratiating.

"If there's anything I can do for you at any time, Mr West, I'll be only too glad, I will really," he said. "Last night was a bit of a shock. I wouldn't have behaved like that if I 'adn't just been woke up, that's the truth." He rubbed his bleary eyes. "I'm sorry I be'aved so badly."

"There is one other job you can do for me," Roger said.

"Anything, Mr West, anything! What is it?"

"I want you to have a look at a man who's been knocked about a bit," said Roger. "You may recognise him."

"Well, I don't know about that," said Tenby, "but I'll see 'im."

Tenby seemed on edge on the way to the City Hospital, but had recovered some of his confidence. Once or twice he rustled some chocolate paper in his pocket.

They walked along the corridors, Tenby complaining that he didn't like the smell of antiseptics: they always made him feel sick; he never went into a hospital unless he was forced to, he declared.

"Nor did this man," said Roger, dryly.

He reached Joe's room, and opened the door without knocking. Joe was sitting up in bed with a newspaper in front of him. He glanced up, and his expression hardened when he saw Roger who entered first.

Then he saw Tenby. There was a flash of recognition in his eyes; only a flash, but quite unmistakable. Roger looked sharply at Tenby, but Tenby's face was blank.

So there was another indication; still not evidence, but another line which might develop. Given a trivial charge against Tenby, they could step up the pressure against him.

Where could he find a charge?

He left Tenby in the hall, eating chocolates, and went along to see Peel, who was conscious, but still drowsy. He was not badly hurt, and the chief effect was from morphia. Peel could only suggest that his flask of tea had been doped.

As Roger left, a little old lady hurried along the passage: Peel's mother, intent on seeing her son.

In the office, Roger still worried about Tenby's sudden change of mood, then put it in the back of his mind, and set to work on other possibilities. He rejected the idea of telling a newspaperman about Raeburn's forthcoming marriage; a leakage would probably be blamed on Eve, and do no good. He was anxious to locate the cottage she had mentioned, and sent out a memorandum to the provincial police.

Eddie Day was inquisitive, and called across the office: "Why should Raeburn want to keep the engagement secret, Handsome?"

"Not feeling well?" asked Roger, sympathetically.

"Now come off it!"

"You shouldn't need to ask," said Roger. "He doesn't want us to realise he's going to marry a woman so that she can't be subpoenaed to give evidence against him."

"Why, of course, that's it!" exclaimed Eddie.

Raeburn put down the telephone, and lit a cigarette. Warrender leaned over the desk in the big office at Raeburn Investments, and Raeburn held out his lighter. Probably no one else would have noticed it, but each was aware of the telltale signs of nervousness in the other. Warrender looked thin, older, and more careworn, but the strain of the past few days had not outwardly affected Raeburn.

"Well?" asked Raeburn, at last.

"I think we shall be able to act soon," said Warrender. "The police called for Tenby late last night, and took him off to the Yard. They didn't keep him long, but they suspect him of the attack on Peel, and will watch him pretty closely now – more closely than they had been doing. He swallowed the bait all right."

"Yes," said Raeburn. "Who *did* attack Peel?"

"I did, after I'd noticed him and telephoned for Tenby," answered Warrender. "You needn't worry, they can't get us for that. I slipped out of a first-floor window at the back, went round to the waste patch, and put a morphia tablet in his tea. It didn't work quick enough, so I caught him from behind. He didn't see me, though, don't worry. Tenby's suspected, and he'll be scared enough to do whatever we want."

"I suppose it's all right," said Raeburn, uneasily. "But you're taking a lot of chances."

"I've got to," Warrender said, very deliberately. "I can't trust anyone else, Paul. There's a new porter at the flat, and I think he works for the police. West is like an India rubber."

"One day I'll get him."

"Forget it," said Warrender, "you'll only be asking for trouble.

All we want is to fool him. We'll send Tenby down to the cottage first, and let Eve go afterward. She'd better arrive just before dark. I'll deal with her, and Tenby will come tearing away for help. I'll intercept him, and give him his faked passport and visa, with enough money to satisfy him. Okay?"

"It ought to be all right," Raeburn conceded.

Warrender took a slip of paper from his pocket, and dropped it on to the desk. "Here's something that will interest you," he said, casually.

Raeburn looked down. It was a scrawled note, threatening to tell the police the truth about Eve Franklin's evidence unless Raeburn paid the writer five thousand pounds. There was no signature, but there were instructions to meet a man wearing a red carnation outside the Palladium the following day.

"That will be identified as Tenby's handwriting," Warrender said, with a smile that did not touch his eyes. "It's a perfect forgery, Paul. When the police come to see us, after Tenby's gone, we'll show it to them, and we'll make out a list of imaginary threats by telephone. We'll get away with it, all right."

"Does Melville know?"

"He does not! No one knows but you and me," said Warrender. "I haven't even told Ma." When Raeburn didn't reply, he went on: "Paul, what's on your mind? You're not yourself this morning."

"I'm myself, all right," Raeburn said. "Someone else isn't, that's the trouble. Your India rubber went to see Eve last night."

"*What!*"

"It worries me, too," admitted Raeburn. He leaned back in his chair, and looked at Warrender through his lashes. "Did you know about it?"

"My God, I didn't!"

"Wasn't someone supposed to be watching the apartment?"

"Tenby fixed that with a woman across the road," answered Warrender. "He said there was always someone in – I was told quickly enough when West first went to see Eve. That's the trouble – it's been the trouble since we started employing Tenby; we can't rely on anyone to do exactly what they're told. But – Eve can handle

West now, can't she?"

"She went home and got tight," Raeburn told him, bluntly. Warrender made no comment, but his lips were tightly compressed. "She says she's sure she didn't tell him anything that mattered, but did tell him about the engagement, and that was plenty. He'll probably hand the story out to the newspapers."

"They'd talk to us before doing much," said Warrender, without conviction. "Anyhow, the *Cry* will let us know if the story's been put around."

"I think you're underrating West now," Raeburn said, quietly. "There would be no general statement. It would be passed on to one paper as a scoop, and West wouldn't choose the *Cry*. The best thing is for me to release the story, and spoil West's move. But we're getting away from the point, George. We must know whenever anyone visits Eve."

"I'll see to that in future," Warrender promised.

"You say that very smoothly, said Raeburn. He stood up and walked toward the little man, staring down at him. "You're going to look after everything, aren't you, George? You aren't going to make any mistakes, now that you're doing everything yourself. I should make sure it's done extremely well."

"It will be," Warrender said, flatly. "Listen to me, Paul. Eve will be killed, so *she* can't talk, and Tenby will fall over himself to get out of the country. It just can't go wrong."

Raeburn thrust his hands into his pockets, and did not look away.

"I don't think we ought to take any risk that Tenby might be caught," he said. "Now that we've gone so far, I think we ought to make a clean sweep of it. Tenby's got to be killed."

"But the whole thing turns on Tenby being framed!" Warrender protested. "If they're both killed, we're bound to be suspected. We must have a scapegoat, Paul. You're worrying about nothing, anyway. Tenby couldn't do us any real harm, only Eve can. *He* killed Tony Brown; we've never been directly involved. He says he saw you kill Halliwell, but his evidence wouldn't stand up on its own. He introduced Eve to us – why, Melville could prepare a case which could get Tenby hanged, and leave us clear. There isn't any doubt about it, Paul, don't make another mistake now."

"Another mistake?" murmured Raeburn.

Warrender flashed: "Yes, another! If you hadn't lost your head and killed Halliwell, none of this would have happened. And you wouldn't let me stop Tenby when I saw he was going too far."

He broke off, shocked by the glitter which appeared in Raeburn's eyes.

"So you haven't much confidence left in me," said Raeburn, very thinly.

"I don't trust your judgment over this."

"I'm beginning to doubt whether I can trust yours in anything," Raeburn said, softly. "We'll talk about it again, later. I'll see you at the flat at half past three."

He made a gesture of dismissal as he went back to his desk, while Warrender looked at him intently: Raeburn ignored that protracted stare, and telephoned the Editor of the *Evening Cry*. He began to give details of the story he wanted to appear in that evening issue concerning his coming marriage to Eve Franklin. Warrender went out, and closed the door softly.

It was obvious at a glance that Eve was nervous. She was wearing two great silver fox furs over a smart two-piece dress as she walked quickly up and down the lounge of the Grosvenor. When she saw Raeburn, she caught her breath; then she went toward him with her hands outstretched.

"You look – wonderful," he greeted her.

So all was well!

"Do I, Paul?"

"Too wonderful to remain single," Raeburn said, his eyes brimming over as if with good humour. "I've decided to tell the newspapers, darling, but we'll fool them one way. I've a special licence in my pocket –"

"Paul!"

"Hush," said Raeburn, squeezing her hand. "We'll get married this afternoon."

"Oh, Paul!"

"And you'll go straight home; no one will be likely to follow you except the police, and it doesn't matter about them," Raeburn said. "Tomorrow afternoon I'll send the Rolls round to you, and you can drive to the cottage. I'll come later in the evening. Happy, darling?"

"It's like – it's like a dream."

"It will be a dream! We won't leave here together, my sweet. Go straight to Caxton Hall, and I'll be there at two o'clock."

A clerk and a porter were the witnesses.

When Raeburn reached his flat after the ceremony, the policeman who was watching outside looked at him long and hard. The porter suspected of being a detective was in the hall, but avoided his eye. Raeburn turned to the lift, and a man darted out of the shadows toward him.

"Mr Raeburn!"

Raeburn swung round, for the voice was familiar, and the face only too familiar: it was Tenby.

"What the devil are you doing here?" Raeburn felt a surge of violent rage as he spoke.

"I've got to 'ave a word with you," muttered Tenby. "It's important or I wouldn't 'ave come. I've just got to. It won't take long."

CHAPTER XXII

TENBY ACCUSES

THE DAMAGE was done, Raeburn thought savagely; Tenby had been seen coming here, and the police would guess whom he had come to see. Raeburn fought to control his feelings. "All right, come along."

He walked to the lift, with Tenby following at his heels, meekly. They did not say a word in the lift because of the porter. Raeburn thought he saw the suspect porter hurrying up the stairs, but could not be sure. There was no sign of the man when they reached the flat.

Raeburn opened the door with a key, and ushered Tenby in. Ma Beesley popped her head out of the room; at sight of Tenby, she raised her hands in shocked dismay. When her smile came back, it looked as if it were glued on.

"Is George in?" Raeburn demanded.

"Why, yes, in the study." Ma actually gaped at Tenby.

Warrender was sitting at the desk, pretending to look through account books. He stared, poker-faced, until he saw Tenby. Then he sprang up. "Good God!"

"It shook me, too," Raeburn said. He slammed the door, then gripped Tenby by the coat, and drew him close. "Why the hell did you come here? You know you're paid to keep away. I'd like to –"

Tenby cringed. "It was the only thing to do, Mr Raeburn. I

couldn't stay away – nor would you, if you thought what *I* think."

"Think? You haven't enough brain to think, you drunken swine."

"Maybe I can think better than you imagine," Tenby retorted, with nervous defiance. "I'm not going to be double-crossed by anyone, not even you, Mr Raeburn. It' wasn't any use asking *you* to come to see me, and I mean to get things straight."

Raeburn released him, and Tenby shrugged his coat into position.

"That's a fine way to treat a man who's worked for you like I 'ave," he muttered. "Anyone would think I was a bit of dirt."

Raeburn looked as if he had difficulty keeping his hands off the man. "Let's hear what you've got to say; now you're here."

Tenby took a newspaper from his pocket, unfolded it, and pointed to a single-column headline, an account in the *Evening Cry* of the attack on Peel. "See that?"

"It's in every evening paper," Warrender barked.

"I dessay it is," said Tenby. "But here's something that ain't. West nearly pulled me for that job."

"I've told you West will catch up with you one day," said Warrender.

"West won't ever catch up with me if I'm, not double crossed," retorted Tenby, softly. "You think I don't know what happened, don't you? Well, I'll tell you something. I was called to Algit last night by a man who *said* he was a friend of mine. I didn't know who it was, and thought it might be you. When I reached the Pump, no one was there to see me. I hung about waiting for a bit, and that's the time when Peel was bashed. I've got no alibi, see? "

Raeburn said: "Well?"

"I couldn't understand it until I read that story," Tenby went on. "Then I knew it was a frame-up, Mr Raeburn. Someone made sure I'd got no alibi, too. It looks to me as if you and your pal George think I'm too dangerous, and want me inside. Let me tell you this, I've got *plenty* to say if I get caught. If West catches up with me on his own, I won't open my trap, but if you fix me – then you'll see what happens."

He stopped, and moistened his lips.

Warrender said: "You're a fool, Tenby," but Tenby was staring at Raeburn, who had been bleak-faced during the first part of the story. Toward the end, he began to smile in a curious fashion, not one that Tenby could dislike.

"If you had an idea like that in your head, it was better to get it out," he said, "but you're wrong, Tenby."

"Then who –"

"I don't know who sent that telephone message, but I do know that we don't want you in the dock." Raeburn spoke derisively. "Where would we be if you were put up in front of a good counsel? Don't be a fool."

"Then who did it?"

"We'll have to find out," said Raeburn.

"Maybe you know where to start," muttered Tenby. The other's attitude obviously both placated and puzzled him. "I'm tired of it, Mr Raeburn, that's the truth. I don't mind admitting I thought I did a good job when I got rid of Brown, but ever since then I've been worried because things just haven't gone right. It's not only the telephone message; it's the other business, too."

"What other business?" Warrender demanded.

"Don't kid me," sneered Tenby. "You know. The Barnes Common do and the affair at Berry Street."

"We want to talk to you about those," said Raeburn. "Perhaps it *is* as well you came. Why did you fix those two jobs?"

"*I* didn't fix 'em!" Tenby looked flabbergasted. "'Ere, what's the game, Mr Raeburn? You've been using others besides me; it's no use pretending you 'aven't. Even last night, there was another bit of mystery. The skirt I got to watch Eve's flat was taken in by a phony message – someone said 'er old man 'ad met with a n'accident, but he 'adn't. Wot *is* all this, Mr Raeburn?"

"Are you trying to pretend you didn't attack Katie Brown –?"

"I've got more sense!"

After a long, tense pause, Raeburn said: "Then who did?" He stared at Warrender, who looked almost frightened; a barrier of suspicion and distrust had risen between them; there was dislike in the way they looked at each other. "I certainly want to know who did," Raeburn went on. "That's something else we'll have to find out, Tenby, but I shouldn't worry too much if I were you."

"That's easy to say, but everywhere I go the dicks are on me tail. It's coming to something when they drag me out of bed for questioning. The truth is it's time I dropped the lot and cleared out."

"You mean out of the country?"

"Out of London would do for a start," Tenby replied, edgily. "Not that I would mind going abroad for a bit. Wot's on your mind, Mr Raeburn?"

"I've a little cottage in Berkshire, not far from Reading, where you'd be all right for a few days," Raeburn said. "It's empty, too. Care to go there?"

"Maybe it's not a bad idea," Tenby conceded. "But understand me, Mr Raeburn; I didn't do the Barnes job or the Berry Street one, neither."

When he left the flat, he had a box of chocolates and the keys of the cottage with him. Raeburn's final injunction was ringing in his ears: he must make the journey after dark, so that the police wouldn't find out where he'd gone.

Turnbull came into Roger's office, next morning, and squatted on the corner of his desk. Roger was opening a letter addressed to M'*sieu l'Inspecteur Roger West,* and glanced up.

"Half a mo'."

"I only want to tell you that Tenby called on Raeburn last night, and Raeburn didn't think much of it."

Roger dropped the letter from France. "When was this?"

"I heard about an hour ago," said Turnbull, swinging his legs. "Raeburn went up in the air when he saw Tenby, but soon cooled off. He took Tenby upstairs, and our little friend came down half an hour later, looking as pleased as Punch – and hugging a box of chocolates!"

"Chocolates," echoed Roger.

"Tenby's got a sweet tooth, remember."

"But still – a box of chocolates from Raeburn to Tenby," said Roger. He paused. "Tenby still being followed by a good man?"

"Yes."

"That's okay." At last, Roger opened the letter from Paris, and his eyes brightened as he read. He pushed the letter across to Turnbull, and was actually grinning. "Ma Beesley used to go around with one tall handsome man, and one small, very thin man," he said. "The Trouville and Deauville police were after them. There's no proof, but strong suspicion, that they were confidence tricksters. I'll ask Raeburn how he likes the twin resorts, one of these days. It can't be coincidence."

"Shouldn't think so, but it doesn't give us what we want," Turnbull said. "Anything else come in?"

"No. I've arranged for Raeburn, Warrender, and Ma to go along to the City Hospital to see Joe," Roger told him. "I had a job to persuade them, but they toed the line. It's a long chance, but we might strike lucky. Any trace of Ma's early London life?"

"She lived way back in a flat in Bethnal Green," said Turnbull, "and her reputation wasn't so hot; she sent her kids out begging, but always managed to keep her nose clean. She left there in 1929."

"How old were the kids?"

"The eldest was about fifteen," said Turnbull. "The others still school age."

"Did you get their names?"

"Not yet, but I'm still trying. What about Raeburn's little cottage in the country?"

"I nearly forgot that," Roger said.

"Yeah?"

Roger shrugged. "We can't very well watch every place that Raeburn owns, but I think there's some funny business over this place where Eve is going. I've located it – not far from Reading. I've asked Mark Lessing to go down there; he was aching for a chance to get his own back." Roger narrowed his eyes, as he went on: "We might withdraw most of our men from open tagging for twelve hours, but keep all Raeburn's associates watched, of course. They might get careless."

"What does Chatworth say?"

"He says that the *Cry's* readers are enough to drive anyone mad, judging from their letters of protest, and he supposes I know what I'm doing," said Roger, flatly. "We'll have them off tomorrow morning. Meanwhile, we'll let Raeburn and his friends see our mysterious Joe. Care to come along?"

"I would!"

"You drive Warrender and Ma, I'll take Raeburn," said Roger. "They're due here any minute. All they know is they're going to see a man suspected of burgling their flat."

The trio were waiting in the hall, Raeburn with obvious impatience, Warrender looking a little shinier, Ma even fatter. During the journey, Raeburn sat silent, smoking cigarette after cigarette. As they reached the Bank, he asked: "Just where are we going, West?"

"Didn't I tell you?" asked Roger, as if surprised. "This man's at the City Hospital. One of our men was knocked about badly the other night, and is also there."

"This business won't take long, I hope?"

"It should be all over in less than twenty minutes," Roger said, mildly.

He took Raeburn into the ward first. Joe was sitting in bed, propped up with pillows. He was a better colour, and looked younger than he had at Berry Street, and during his first few days at the hospital. The bald patch at the front of his head added years to his appearance; he was probably in the early thirties.

Joe looked at Raeburn blankly.

"Have you ever seen this man before, Mr Raeburn?" Roger asked.

"No," answered Raeburn, flatly. "Never."

Nothing in his expression suggested that he was lying, and there was no flash of recognition between the two.

"And I certainly don't know *him*" Joe said. "I'm a stranger to millionaires who get their names in the papers.'*

"Is that all?" asked Raeburn, coldly.

"Wait outside for a few minutes, please, while the others come

169

in," Roger said.

Turnbull brought Warrender in, a lion with a black sheep. Warrender gave the impression that he was afraid of a trap, and looked relieved when, after a prolonged stare at the man on the bed, he said: "I don't think this was one of the men who burgled the flat. In fact, I'm sure it wasn't."

"Right, thanks," said Roger, briskly. "Mrs Beesley, please," he called.

Ma Beesley came in. She grinned inanely about her, but on the instant Joe's expression changed and for a second there was recognition in his eyes. It quickly disappeared, and there was no change at all in Ma's manner, but Roger was convinced that these two knew each other.

Outside the hospital, a newsboy stood selling papers. Raeburn bought an *Evening Cry,* and Roger followed suit, wondering whether news of the engagement had leaked out. The first headline to catch his eye ran: PAUL RAEBURN WED.

Roger looked up into Raeburn's face.

"Aren't you going to congratulate me?" the millionaire asked, smoothly.

CHAPTER XXIII

REPORT FROM LALEHAM

COTTAGE

MARK LESSING reached the Berkshire village at lunch time, and drew his Talbot up in the gravelled courtyard of The King's Arms. It was drizzling, and the sky was very dark in the east; a bleak wind was blowing, and there was little about the weather or the countryside to cheer him. The low-built inn needed painting, and might be drab. He had driven through the village, and found it equally depressing. It was off the main road, and the local inhabitants seemed to take little pride in their homes. Nearly opposite the inn was a garage, outside which stood several derelict cars and some rusty petrol pumps.

Mark had to bend low in order to get into the hall of the inn. He stood for some minutes, but no one appeared. He pushed open two doors marked SALOON and LOUNGE, but both rooms were deserted. He could hear voices from the back of the inn, and, going to another closed door, he pushed it open and called: "Anyone about?"

"Whassat?" a man asked, almost from underneath his nose.

He looked down to see a little wizened creature, with overlong hair, staring at him.

"Can I get some lunch?"

"Lunch?" the man echoed, as if the word were new to him. "Well, now, I don't know if there's anything left."

"Bread and cheese, and a glass of beer would do."

"I daresay we can fix something. Just go through the lounge," said the little man.

The lounge had not been tidied up since the previous night's occupation. The ash trays were full, and the dried marks of wet glasses showed on the tables. The grey ashes of a long-dead fire looked cheerless in a small grate. Mark had started out cheerfully and hopefully, but this was enough to damp anybody's spirits.

He pushed open a door marked DINING ROOM, and light from a blazing fire in a large grate made him blink. The room was warm. Several people sat at the small tables, and everyone looked up at him. Most of them had reached the sweet course.

No one was there to take his order, so he went to a table near the fire and looked at a finger-soiled menu card. The pencilled offering was 'Roast Beef. He glanced toward the service door; at last it opened, and the little man came in, carrying a plate of soup.

He made a beeline for Mark. "You're lucky, sir," he announced, proudly.

"That's good."

"Beef to follow," went on the wizened man. "Anything to drink?"

"A pint of beer, please."

The pint came in a battered pewter tankard, but the brew was good. So were the roast beef, the rich Yorkshire pudding, and even the Brussels sprouts. Mark's spirits rose as he set to. He was the last in the dining-room, except the little man who stood warming his back and looking at him as he ate.

"Passing through?" the man asked at last.

"Yes and no," said Mark, and told his prepared lie. "I'm looking for a house."

"Not the only one," said the little man. "Shocking, the shortage is. Large or small?"

"Medium."

"Don't know of one." The little man shook his head. "Might

have more luck in Reading, but I doubt it."

"I'm looking for a place in the country," Mark explained, "and I thought I'd stay here for a night or two. You have a room, I suppose?"

"Could do it," conceded the little man. "We've got several rooms, if it comes to that. Show you the best one after lunch."

He became positively garrulous when they left the dining-room, and was soon chatting about Laleham Cottage; Mark's errand had reminded him of it. The cottage had changed hands some months before, but no one had come to live there. Oh, yes, it was furnished. It was a crying shame that people bought houses and left them empty, while others had nowhere to live. The cottage was just over there – he pointed out of a front bedroom window as a matter of fact, it had five bedrooms and three rooms downstairs, as well as a couple of acres. Some cottage!

The house was built halfway up a bleak hill, and about half a mile away. Beyond the building, the hill was wooded, and at one side was a dark patch of shrubs.

"I know what it's like, because I had a look round when it was up for sale," explained the little innkeeper. "Six thousand five hundred – I'd rather keep my money in the bank! Well, how does this room suit you?"

"I think I'm going to like it," said Mark.

The weather cleared in the middle of the afternoon, and he went to look at Raeburn's new place. No one was about. The grounds were well kept and the ornamental garden trim and well stocked. The house was attractive from the outside, mainly Elizabethan, but one or two recent alterations had been made.

On a wide lawn, in the front garden, stood a summerhouse and Mark strolled toward it. From its window he could see the house and the long drive; he could not want a better place in which to conceal himself.

"It'll do me for tonight," he decided, and drove back to The King's Arms. He was determined to succeed down here, whatever it cost; the Brighton fiasco rankled.

Just before dark, he took the car rugs to the summerhouse, and made sure that the cottage was still unoccupied. He went back to the inn for dinner, which was as good as lunch had been, deciding to begin his vigil immediately afterward. He walked to the summer-house, and settled down.

By nine o'clock he was cold and cramped. To get warm, he strode about the lawn, looking down on the village and its few lights, and, farther away, toward the myriad yellow dots, the lights of Reading. The wind had strengthened, and cut right through him.

"I wonder how long I need stay?" he asked himself.

If anyone arrived at the house, lights would go on, and he would be able to see them from his room window. He decided to end the vigil at midnight, had another brisk walk to get warm, and returned to the summer-house.

At half past eleven, he heard a car approaching. He got up, and went to the window. The headlights were shining on the house, and, as the car turned into the drive, shone toward him. Mark ducked. The light passed him, bathing the house in its glare. He could not see clearly, but felt sure there were two people in the car.

"Raeburn and his Eve, perhaps." He felt the sharp edge of excitement. "I – no, it isn't!"

Two men appeared in the headlights, and Mark saw something pass between them; the car was a taxi, and there was only one passenger. It was a man, who stood on the porch as the taxi turned for the return journey, and Mark recognised him immediately from photographs.

It was Tenby.

Tenby opened the front door and went inside; a light blazed out from the hall. The front door closed, and other lights went on, first at the front, and then at the sides. Mark could see the man moving about.

He ventured out of the summer-house, but could neither hear nor see anyone near. He approached the cottage cautiously, and saw Tenby in a front room with a bottle and a glass by his side.

Tenby got up, yawning. He opened a box of chocolates, popped one into his mouth, picked up the box, and went out of the room, switching off the light. His footsteps sounded heavily on the stairs.

Mark hurried back to the village, and telephoned Roger, at home.

"Couldn't be better," Roger said. "We'd lost him...."

Stay in your room, or the hotel, until we're in touch. We'll be watching, but may not show ourselves until tomorrow."

"Right," Mark said, and went back and treated himself to a double Scotch.

He was in his room next evening, looking out of the window, when a small car stopped outside the garage.

The driver, small, square-shouldered, vaguely familiar, got out to look for an attendant. He had a heavy black beard and moustache, and was wearing a cloth cap and a tweed coat, so obviously theatrical that it seemed absurd.

The garage attendant appeared, wiping his hands on an oily rag. "And what can I do for you, sir?"

"Petrol and oil," said the bearded man, brusquely.

Mark stood watching, trying to place his voice, watched him pay the attendant, get back into the car, and drive toward Laleham Cottage. He went past the gateway, turned right at the top of a hill just beyond the cottage, and disappeared behind a copse of beech. Mark heard the gears change. Then the sound of the engine faded.

For a while nothing happened, and no one appeared. Mark began to wonder whether Roger had been right to tell him to stay here, when he saw the theatrical-looking man hurry, across a patch of grass, and disappear again behind some dark shrubs. Mark could see his hat bobbing up and down, as if he were trying to reach the cottage without being seen.

A car came along the village High Street, making little sound; Mark first saw it out of the corner of his eye. He drew in a sharp breath as he recognised Raeburn's Silver Wraith, with a woman at the wheel; no one was with her.

"And Eve makes three," Mark murmured. "Now I'll make four."

He hurried downstairs, putting on his coat as he went. His car was standing in the yard. The self-starter did not work at the first push, and he growled at it; promptly the engine hummed. As he turned into the road, he could think only of one thing: the bearded man's furtive approach and its possible significance. He might be intent only on hearing what passed between Eve and Tenby, but did the girl know that Tenby was there?

Mark saw one of two men who had been in the hotel for lunch, near the entrance to the cottage grounds; the man was concealed from the house by trees. Mark waved to him casually, and drove on in the direction taken by the bearded man. The little car was parked off the road near the copse. He pulled up a few yards farther along, jumped out, and hurried across the open ground where he had seen the man. It seemed a long way to the cottage, and his heart was thumping. He could not see his quarry, but as he reached the drive and peered through the bushes, he saw Eve standing at the front door, which had just been opened, and heard her exclaim: *"You!"*

"Well, wot a pleasure," Tenby said, in a high-pitched voice. "Wot a pleasure it is, Evie. I never thought I'd see you 'ere. What's the game?"

"What are you doing here?" Eve demanded, shrilly.

"I've been invited," Tenby answered, grandly. "My wealthy friends decided I was socially okay, but I didn't know anyone else was coming."

They went in.

Mark crept round to the back of the cottage, and tried the back door; it was not locked. He stepped inside, keeping a sharp look out for the bearded man. He saw the marks made by damp shoes on the oil cloth, and went into a narrow passage which presumably led from the kitchen to the front of the house. He passed a door which he thought was closed.

He was about to go into the hall, when a hand shot out from the door, without any warning, and clutched his throat, stifling a cry. He caught a glimpse of the man with the black beard; then a sharp blow caught him behind the ear, and he felt his senses swimming.

The bearded man broke his fall, left him lying on the floor, and opened the door wider.

Tenby had been talking shrilly all the time, and now his voice was clear; Mark could just hear him! "It's a trap, that's what it is, a trap. Don't ask me who they want to trap, the ruddy swine!"

"What – what are you going to do?" asked Eve, in a scared voice.

"I'm going to ring Raeburn, that's what." There were quick footsteps as he crossed the hall, and the bearded man crept toward it. Tenby banged the receiver up and down, and Mark, trying to get up without attracting attention, sensed the desperate anxiety in the man's voice as he cried: "For Gawd's sake, answer me!"

"Is – is it working?" asked Eve.

"It's nothing but a bloody trap!" cried Tenby. "'Ere, I'm getting out. I never trusted the swine. I even kept me case packed. Get out of my way."

"Don't leave me alone!" There was terror in Eve's voice. "Tenby, don't –"

Mark heard a thud, as if Tenby had pushed her against the wall. Then the front door slammed. Mark tried to get up again, but the pain in his head was agonising, and he dared not make a noise.

The bearded man crept forward, out of his sight.

Then Mark, trying again, saw Roger West stepping silently along the passage. Roger glanced at him, winked, and put a finger to his lips.

In the hall, Eve was pulling at the front door, the bearded man was creeping up on her, and Roger waited, Out of sight, ready to move on the instant.

Eve was pulling at the front door, terrified now that Tenby had gone. She saw and heard nothing behind her, but the man with the beard crept toward her, holding a scarf stretched out. He moved suddenly, dropped it over her head, and pulled tightly.

Her cry was strangled to silence. The scarf dropped to her neck, and the bearded, man began to pull it tighter, unaware that anyone else was at the door.

"Not quick enough, Warrender," Roger observed, mildly. "And not fast enough, either."

Roger moved very fast indeed, and as the man with the theatrical beard swung round, he ran into Roger's fist, and sagged back against the wall.

Roger bent over Eve, untied the scarf, and said: "Now take it easy, Evie, you'll be all right. And even if we can't pin murder on to him, Warrender will get ten years in jail for attacking you,"

"Warrender!" the girl exclaimed.

"Plus beard," Roger explained, easily. "Ten years for attempted murder," he said," and we'll probably make the capital charge stick, Warrender." He leaned forward, and tugged at the black beard; it sagged loose, with a soft tearing sound. "Mark!" he called, and turned to see Mark coming unsteadily into the hall "Look after Eve, will you?"

"So you had to do it yourself," Mark said, weakly.

"I took the tailers off Warrender, and he thought he'd been clever enough to evade them," Roger explained. "He didn't realise we were reporting his progress by radio every few miles, or that we were waiting here for him. You must have given him a bit of a shock."

Warrender just stood there, like a man damned.

"I don't pretend to know all the answers yet," said Roger to Turnbull, "but we're getting on, Warren. Eve either can't or won't talk, Warrender won't, and Tenby's pretending to be half asleep, but they'll all talk when the time comes. It's clear that Warrender planned to kill Eve, and to frame Tenby. He would probably have killed Mark, too, and let Tenby take the rap for that as well, if he'd got away with it. Taking the tabs off him was a good move."

"Seen the AC?" asked Turnbull. "He ought to have a *billet-doux* ready for the Home Secretary."

"Give me a chance, I haven't been back twenty minutes," said Roger. "I want a talk with Raeburn before I see Chatworth, anyhow."

He was going through reports on his desk when a superintendent looked in.

"Oh, West," he said, "the Assistant Commissioner would like to see you." He paused, and then delivered his bombshell: "Mr Paul Raeburn is with him."

CHAPTER XXIV

RAEBURN MAKES A STATEMENT

CHATWORTH WAS sitting behind his desk, puffing at a small cigar. Raeburn was in one of the tubular steel armchairs, his hat, gloves and stick on the floor by his side, his ankles crossed. His expression was one of complete assurance, and he smiled affably as Roger entered, but made no attempt to rise.

"Ah, West," said Chatworth. He paused as Roger, schooling himself to show no emotion, approached the desk. "Mr Raeburn has come to make a statement."

"Has he, sir?"

"It's one which, I hope, will help to clear up the misunderstanding between us," Raeburn said, urbanely. "As I have told Sir Archibald, I have been very worried about your attitude, Chief Inspector. Only now do I realise that you had very good reason for being suspicious of my actions."

"Oh," said Roger, blankly.

Chatworth said: "Sit down, West."

"Thank you, sir," Roger said, as he sat down. His mind was beginning .to work, searching for the trick behind this bold move.

"I hope that I'm in time to make sure that nothing more goes wrong." Raeburn said. "I've had a very great shock, Chief Inspector. A man whom I trusted implicitly has betrayed me." He smiled faintly. "I'm afraid this sounds, rather dramatic, but it is the simple truth."

Was he positive that Warrender would not talk? Could he be? Or was he preparing his defence against betrayal?

"I think I ought to tell you that when I first met Warrender, he actually swindled me out of several hundred pounds," Raeburn said, very carefully, "I caught him, and he pleaded for another chance. I gave it to him. I believe in trying to help lame dogs over stiles, Chief Inspector. Since then, he has always worked competently for me, and I believed loyally. I had almost forgotten the curious nature of our first meeting until this shocking discovery."

"I see," said Roger, heavily.

"During the past few days, I have been worried by telephone calls and messages from a man named Tenby," Raeburn went on. "Tenby is a man whom Warrender employed for several jobs in connection with my greyhound racing tracks, when I first opened them. I had met him, although I hardly remembered him. The messages were all very much alike; he threatened me with some disastrous disclosure. What the disclosure was he didn't say, and I certainly couldn't guess. The man actually came to see me yesterday afternoon, Chief Inspector."

"Did he?" asked Roger, and thought helplessly that this man had genius – a genius for evil distortion.

Chatworth sat impassive.

"Yes, Tenby came to see me," Raeburn repeated. "Warrender was present, and obviously Tenby was not at his ease. It transpired that he hoped to blackmail me because –" he paused, and leaned forward impressively – "because Eve Franklin did *not* see the accident when Halliwell was killed. Tenby had forced her to say that she had, as part of his scheme of blackmail."

This was really brilliant: a smooth answer to every charge, even before it was made, but *could* he be sure of Warrender?

"When I realised that there was reason to doubt the truth of the evidence, I was well able to understand your attitude," said Raeburn, spreading his hands. "It was a complete surprise to me to discover that Eve had committed perjury. You know that I fell in love with her – that we were married yesterday. This news shocked me beyond words. It was difficult to believe, yet Tenby convinced me of its truth. I at once began to make inquiries. My wife does not admit that she lied to save me, but I gather from her manner that she is troubled. Consequently, I arranged for her to visit a cottage I own near Reading, promising to join her there later. I thought that, during a quiet week-end, I would be more likely to learn the truth.

"I am quite sure of this," Raeburn went on, leaning forward again. "If she did commit perjury, it was under someone's influence. This man Tenby first introduced her to Warrender. I believe that Tenby found a way to dominate Eve, and to make her come forward as she did. My faith in my wife is absolutely unshaken."

Melville would talk to Warrender and to Eve, of course; certainly, Raeburn must be absolutely sure of himself – unless this was a bluff to out-do all bluffs.

Chatworth asked, like a cigar-smoking Buddha: "What inquiries did you make?"

"I asked my housekeeper, Mrs Beesley, to find out what she could," Raeburn told him. "She knew Warrender before I met him, and has never been as confident of his loyalty as I have." Raeburn sighed, just enough to suggest that he was still suffering from the shock of betrayal. "You see, gentlemen, I read of the brutal attack on the Brown woman the other evening. I remembered the supposedly accidental death of Tony Brown. I knew – who could fail to know – that, in your mind, all these things would be connected? I hoped that I would be able to show that there was no connection, but I'm afraid that there was."

He paused for effect.

He appeared slightly disappointed at the stony reception of his news; he glanced from Roger to Chatworth and back again, and for the first time he showed some signs of disquiet. When he went on, it was in a harder voice.

"I am afraid that Warrender was behind these vicious crimes which were committed partly to cover up the fact that he had persuaded my wife to commit perjury, partly to be able to blackmail me at a later date. It seems evident to me now that my wife's ex-fiancé, Tony Brown, knew of that. Did you ever suspect that he was *murdered,* gentlemen?"

Roger felt sick.

"It did occur to us," Chatworth said, heavily.

"I am afraid it is true, too." Raeburn stood up and began to pace the room. "There is another thing. Tenby accused me of luring him to Aldgate the other evening, so that he would be framed – I quote him – for the attack on the policeman Peel. I accused Warrender of this. He denied it, of course, but there was no doubt that Warrender was gravely troubled by Tenby's visit, and by my suspicions. Mrs Beesley, Mr Melville, and I were talking about it most of the night."

Melville, with a good counsel, could convince any jury of this story. Raeburn was actually giving a preview of his defence.

Now he thought it wise to seem on edge.

"You *must* try to understand the distress which I felt," he went on, earnestly. "I had no proof, only suspicion, and Warrender tried to convince me that those suspicions were baseless."

"What made you come here now?" Roger forced himself to ask.

"Mrs Beesley telephoned me only a little while ago, and told me that Warrender had left the flat by the fire escape, last night, although I had ordered him to stay there until I returned." So Raeburn was going to pretend that he did not know of Warrender's arrest. "Mrs Beesley is a very shrewd woman, as no doubt you know, and she had been keeping a watchful eye on him for some time. She found a slip of paper in his coat last night – yes, she entered his room, and searched his pockets while he was asleep. The note makes it clear that Warrender and Tenby were planning this blackmail together. Would you like to know my final conclusions, gentlemen?"

"Very much," said Roger, heavily.

"I think that Warrender has been using my name and my companies as a cover for extensive criminal operations." Raeburn stood in front of Chatworth; his eyes were flashing, a most plausible imitation of a man in great distress. "I think that I have been completely deceived by a very clever rogue. Mrs Beesley suspected this some time ago, but wanted to be sure before she spoke. It seems evident that Warrender has reason to fear that his activities would be discovered. He was afraid that, if I were convicted of manslaughter, the police would investigate my affairs and, necessarily, his. I think he created a situation which eventually grew too big for him, and in desperation resorted to murder, and to hiring dangerous criminals to cover his tracks.

"You will ask what grounds I have for these suspicions. I can only say –" Raeburn hesitated, and then threw up his hands. "I can only say that the facts are clear to me now that I have been through my books. Warrender has been robbing me of huge sums. He had access to my banking accounts, and you will find that the figures speak for themselves. I know that I was wrong to trust him, but that is not the point now. I *did* trust him." Raeburn spoke as if he were righteousness itself. "Gentlemen, I want you to make the fullest inquiry into my affairs wherever Warrender has been connected with them. I want the whole truth to come out. No matter how hurtful, I will face it. Warrender's departure from the flat seems to me an admission of guilt. I want you to find him, too; he may have made plans to leave the country."

"That's possible," Chatworth grunted, as if he had to make some contribution.

"I can only hope you will get results quickly," Raeburn went on, briskly. "I really cannot carry on working until everything is known." He put his hand into his pocket, drew out a key case, and dropped it on to the desk. "These are the keys to my safe at the flat, and to my strong room at the company offices. You may examine everything at your leisure. No doubt you expect Warrender to try to wriggle out of this, and no doubt he will try to smear me with his own dirt, but – "

"Mr Raeburn," Roger interrupted, in a deceptively quiet voice, "this isn't going to work out quite as you expected. There's something I don't think you know. Warrender failed to kill your wife. He is now under arrest, charged with attempted murder. Your wife –"

Raeburn put out a hand on a chair to steady himself.

"You mean he tried to *murder* Eve?" he cried. "He wanted to kill *her* to stop her from saying anything that might harm him. She – she isn't hurt?" He jumped forward, gripping Roger's arm. "Tell me that she isn't hurt."

Did he really think he could get away with all this? Could he?

A telephone bell rang on Chatworth's desk, breaking the tension. Chatworth picked up the instrument, growled: "Chatworth," and then actually gasped. "No!" Roger was watching Raeburn, and saw the momentary glint of triumph in his eyes.

Chatworth barked: "Who'd seen him? . . . Melville? ... Yes, I see." He rang off, and stared at Roger who was at screaming pitch.

"No doubt you expected this, Mr Raeburn," he said. "Your solicitor visited Warrender in his cell. After he had left, Warrender died of potassium of cyanide poisoning. It appears to have been contained in a false heel of his shoe."

"Why, that is terrible," Raeburn said, and it sounded like a song of triumph.

"Whether Melville got the cyanide to him, whether it was murder or suicide, I don't think we'll ever know," Roger said, bleakly. "I do know that Raeburn's story will stand up in court, now. We still can't charge him."

That afternoon, Joe volunteered a statement. In it Warrender was shown as the man who had hired him to commit all his crimes – against Katie Brown and against Brown himself.

Their only remaining hopes were Tenby and Eve. Whatever Eve knew, she could not be forced into the witness box; so Tenby, still at Reading, was the one hope.

That afternoon, Tenby was rushed to the Royal Berkshire Hospital, but died before he got there – of morphine poisoning.

CHAPTER XXV

THE TRUTH ABOUT JOE

Get ME Reading Police Headquarters," Roger ordered, soon after he heard of Tenby's death, and put the receiver down. "I think I've got a line, sir," he said to Chatworth, very quietly. "Tenby came out of Raeburn's flat carrying a box of chocolates, and I always thought that was odd, I'll ask Reading to find that box; it's probably at the cottage. If the post-mortem shows chocolate and morphine in the stomach, we can act."

"You'd still have to prove that Raeburn poisoned them." "Even proving he bought or could have touched them will be a help. He might have fingered the box, too; and one fragmentary print on one chocolate would do the trick. We know he's our man; all we need is a break to push him over."

The telephone bell rang.

"Excuse me, sir . . . Oh, yes, Turnbull."

Roger listened to Turnbull, who was obviously in one of his rare moments of excitement.

"*Now* I've got something for you," he said. "I've traced Ma Beesley's eldest son." There was a long pause and Roger could have shouted at him. "A gentleman named Joe," he finished, gloatingly.

"Joe!"

"Joe," Turnbull crowed. "He deserted from the Army, and has been dodging about the East End for years. And I've got something

185

even better."

"You couldn't have."

"Couldn't I? This Joe's been in touch with Ma Beesley – a landlady at the house he stayed at described her to a T. They've met within the last month."

"I'm going to see Joe, right away," said Roger, softly. "And pray for results from the p.m. on Tenby."

The post-mortem report came through an hour later: Roger read it with increasing excitement. There was chocolate in Tenby's stomach, with a strong concentration of morphine.

The box of chocolates had been found in his luggage, and each chocolate analysed; several contained morphine which had been injected into them.

"Get every chocolate tested for prints," urged Roger. "Get every one photographed and blown up; we've got to get a fingerprint."

Raeburn stayed in Reading until Eve was taken away from The King's Arms by the police. On the return journey he looked very grave, and when he reached Park Lane, he found newspapermen and photographers waiting. After he had faced the battery of flashlights, and been asked for an interview, he shook his head slowly.

"I'm sorry, boys. This has been a gruelling time for me, and I'd rather not say anything just now." He resisted all their pressure, waved his hat, gave rather a melancholy smile, and went up in the lift.

Ma Beesley opened the door of the flat.

"Welcome back, Paul," she said, and stood aside for him to pass. She showed her ugly teeth in a grin as she closed the door. "Maud's out," she went on, "so we're here on our own. Everything's all right, then?"

The grave look had vanished from Raeburn's face. He was grinning, and with almost boyish glee took her face between his hands, and kissed her soundly. "Everything's fine, Ma! We're going to get away with it, thanks to you and Abel."

"Abel's decided not to come and see us for a day or two," Ma told him, and watched him very carefully. "There's only one thing I don't get, Paul. How did you manage to kill Tenby?"

"He was too fond of chocolates," Raeburn gloated. "I gave him a big box before he left here, with doped ones in the bottom layer. I knew he wouldn't eat them until he got to the cottage."

Ma said: "Very smart, I agree, but supposing he'd eaten the doped ones too soon?"

"Would it really have mattered?" asked Raeburn. "The police would have felt sure he was murdered; now they think it was suicide – that's the only difference. I wanted him dead, and wanted Warrender to attack Eve. He was close on her heels, and even if she'd found Tenby dead, Warrender would have gone in to kill her; the police were bound to be at hand to catch him red-handed – as they did."

"Supposing he *had* killed her, Paul?"

"As you'd telephoned West and warned him to watch Eve, I didn't think there was much risk," said Raeburn, carelessly. "If he had – " he shrugged. "Oh, forget it. You've done magnificently, Ma, a lot of credit's due to you."

"I even managed to convince you that Eve is loyal," said Ma, "and I let poor George think I agreed with him about killing her. But you thought the whole thing out, Paul, I have to admit that. Did you have it in mind when you ran over Halliwell?"

"Oh, not as far back as that," Raeburn admitted. "It was when I was in the dock, realizing that it might catch up with me sometime, that I began to plan a way out. The obvious thing was to put the blame on George. Only you and Tenby could have disproved it, and I knew I could rely on you."

"I've never *really* liked George," Ma wheezed.

Raeburn was looking dreamily at the door. "Yes, it all began while I was in the dock. I wonder what West would say to that! It was a remark you made about your son Joe being on the run from the Army authorities which gave me the idea of letting him do some work that Tenby would be blamed for, too. Obviously, that would sow suspicion between Tenby and George – and be the real beginning. The details worked themselves out as we went along.

When Tenby murdered Tony Brown, I could see that it was coming along nicely. Bill Brown nearly upset the applecart, but you and Joe were equal to the occasion, Ma! By going after Bill Brown, letting himself be caught, and naming Warrender on the day agreed, Joe put the finishing touch to everything. And you did remarkably well when you interviewed Eve; you certainly proved her loyalty. I had to be quite sure of that."

"Such a lovely girl," cooed Ma.

"And how that interview confused West," Raeburn exulted. "Well, it's all over, Ma, and now I can concentrate on politics. When the police go into the accounts –"

"They'll find I've cooked them beautifully," crowed Ma. "I've made them look as if that wicked George has been fleecing you right and left."

Raeburn chuckled, delightedly. "And under his very nose! But getting Joe to agree to serve a long sentence was the deciding factor, Ma. I won't forget it."

"I'm sure you won't," said Ma. "And you won't forget the fifty thousand pounds you're going to put aside for him when he comes out, will you? But don't worry about that now, Paul, you must be tired. Shall I get you a drink?"

"Get *us* a drink!"

The front doorbell rang on Raeburn's words,

"Now I wonder who that is," said Ma. "I'll go."

She hurried to the door, with Raeburn smiling at her back.

His smile faded suddenly when Ma opened the door, and he saw West and Turnbull, with another plain clothes man, standing massively outside.

"Good afternoon, Ma," greeted Roger, and pushed past her into the hall. "Good afternoon, Mr Raeburn."

"What is it now?" Raeburn was sharp.

"We've come for you," Roger said, quietly. "Ma's son, Joe, couldn't keep as silent as he meant to; the fact that he was making himself an accessory to Halliwell's murder made him speak. That's put Ma in a nasty spot. In the second place, you weren't careful enough with Tenby's chocolates. We found a print on a poisoned one from your left index finger. In the third –"

"You're lying!" cried Raeburn, and he went deathly white.

"And in the third place, Eve has also talked," finished Roger, "so we've got you for Halliwell's murder. I convinced her that Warrender went to kill her with your knowledge, and she didn't think much of it. Don't make a fuss," he went on, sardonically, "you'll get your picture in the *Cry*, and probably the readers will write to you in jail."

When Roger got home that night, Janet, the boys, and Mark were all waiting, eager to talk.

"I always *knew* you'd win," Richard crowed.

"It was pretty obvious, wasn't it?" Scoopy declared "Good old pop!"

JOHN CREASEY

GIDEON'S DAY

Gideon's day is a busy one. He balances family commitments with solving a series of seemingly unrelated crimes from which a plot nonetheless evolves and a mystery is solved.

One of the most senior officers within Scotland Yard, George Gideon's crime solving abilities are in the finest traditions of London's world famous police headquarters. His analytical brain and sense of fairness is respected by colleagues and villains alike.

'The finest of all Scotland Yard series' – New York Times.

GIDEON'S FIRE

Commander George Gideon of Scotland Yard has to deal successively with news of a mass murderer, a depraved maniac, and the deaths of a family in an arson attack on an old building south of the river. This leaves little time for the crisis developing at home ....

'Gideon of Scotland Yard emerges as one of the most real working detectives in modern fiction.... A sympathetic and believable professional policeman.' - New York Times

JOHN CREASEY

THE CREEPERS

"The prisoner's hand was thin and bony ... And in the centre of the palm was a pinkish mark. It was the shape of a wolf's head, mouth open, fangs showing. Although it was what he had expected to see, Inspector West felt a twinge of repugnance a stab not unrelated to fear. It was the fifth time he had seen the mark of the wolf – the mark of Lobo."

A gang of cat burglars led by Lobo cause mayhem as they terrorize the city. They must be stopped, but with little in the way of evidence the police are baffled. Just how can Inspector West manage to do this in what is a race against time before more victims succumb?

"Here is an excellent novel of law enforcement officers, harried, discouraged and desperately fatigued, moving inexorably ahead under the pressure of knowledge that they must succeed to save human lives." - Cleveland Plain-Dealer

"Furiously exciting" - Chicago Tribune

"The action is fast, continuous and exciting" - San Francisco News

JOHN CREASEY

THE HOUSE OF THE BEARS

Standing alone in the bleak Yorkshire Moors is Sir Rufus Marne's 'House of the Bears'. Dr. Palfrey is asked to journey there to examine an invalid - who has now disappeared. Moreover, Marne's daughter lies terribly injured after a fall from the minstrel's gallery which Dr. Palfrey discovers was no accident. He sets out to investigate and the results surprise even him . . . .

"'Palfrey' and his boys deserve to take their places among the immortals." - Western Mail

INTRODUCING THE TOFF

Whilst returning home from a cricket match at his father's country home, the Honourable Richard Rollison - alias The Toff - comes across an accident which proves to be a mystery. As he delves deeper into the matter with his usual perseverance and thoroughness , murder and suspense form the backdrop to a fast moving and exciting adventure.

'The Toff has been promoted to a place of honour among amateur detectives.' – The Times Literary Supplement